The Sword of the Gray Queen 3:

Scourge of the Son

Samuel Fleming

For Mom and Dad.

Thanks for always supporting me

and believing in me.

Contents

"Wicked things follow in the
path of the righteous."
—ENCHIRIDION:
Quod Intus Viget Tenebris.
Daemonium, Chapter 4.

Prologue

IT WAS A night for celebration.

Varney Barris licked his lips and strolled the city cobbles, tasting the last of his blood-spiked wine. He threaded between the still crowded streets of Arkcaster, long coat trailing behind him, and enjoying the cool night air on his undead face.

Three glasses of wine had been perfect. "Just perfect," Varney said to himself.

In his mirth, he spun around and took one last look at the block of buildings. It didn't look like much from the outside—a tailor's storefront on one end, a cobbler's storefront on the other—but through the secret entrance and beneath the two stores lay *Les Enfants Terribles* blood den.

A wretched hive of temptation and skullduggery. A place where vampyres, sympathetic elves and humans, and other *less-savory* Terrans could gamble and get a bite to drink.

And that one was now *his* blood den.

Varney smiled and continued down the street.

He knew his stroke of good fortune was, in part, to the misfortune of the previous owner, Marcus Wuanti. Varney also admitted that there were no less than five other vampyres that could've gotten the job. He chalked it up to his diligence and personality.

Pay your dues and pay your respects, kids, and someday you too will move up in the world.

And grovel. A little groveling never hurt anyone.

Varney smiled and muttered a thanks to whatever accident had befallen poor Marcus. It could've been any number of things—the poor sod was still missing and his body hadn't been found. Personally, Varney believed that Marcus had either got caught cheating on his mistress or had offended the master. Either of those could catch a man a slight case of death.

Speaking of…

The moon was high in the sky and the air was crisp. Varney licked his lips. He was already feeling *hungry* again.

"Once you pop the cork, eh?" Varney said to no one in particular.

It was the perfect evening to head to his old hunting ground. He'd been a good lad, after all. He deserved a treat.

~

Varney turned the corner of Westmisson and Eighth. He'd practically skipped along the whole seven blocks like a boy after they'd rung the school bell.

Maybe the blood-spiked wine had been stronger than he thought.

He quickly pushed the thought aside.

Of course, he was still of mind enough to hunt. It would take much more wine than that to deter him. He might not have been the suavest hunter at the moment, but he was going to get his hunger sated.

His old hunting was between the butcher's blocks and shanties on the East side. This side of Arkcaster had been built as an afterthought, a hastily erected section built to accommodate the swelling population of the refugees that came from across the realm during the time of Sircius Everdeath's one lich crusade. After Everdeath disappeared, the population on the East side thinned somewhat and there was never a desire to build more permanent structures.

Varney walked through the criss-crossing streets of his hunting ground, minding the runoff from chamber pots and ducking beneath scrapwood roofs that jutted out at odd heights and lengths. A hog squealed across the street and the shouts of drunkards carried over from the bars. Varney pushed aside the smell of filth, animals, and mildewing wood, focusing on sweat and blood.

His steps had slowed until he felt like he was skulking through a slum jungle. Varney's heart beat with the excitement of his second life—his gifted life.

The smell of salty sweat hung in the air. The faintest promise of copper. Of blood. There was prey to be had here, but was prepared to wait—for the right target, for the right moment.

Varney smiled. *Yes, it was a good night.*

Dare he think: *A good omen.*

Varney heard his prey before he smelled them. A hog squealed in the distance. Shortly after came the sound of tearing flesh, crunch of bone, and the trickle of blood. Varney only heard this because of his heightened senses.

A butcher working late, perhaps?

The vampyre smirked. Maybe there'd be enough left of the hog for a drink. It was a dirty thought, akin to sacrilege in some circles and mere debauchery in others, but Varney was caught up in the moment.

He crept closer, threading his way through the alleys, all the while following and savoring the wet sounds of slaughter. Spittle dripped from his mouth.

Finally, he found the slaughterhouse. It was a wood cabin, only a little more solid than the ramshackle barns and dwellings that lined it. The sounds of slaughter grew lounder.

Varney's excitement had grown to a fever pitch—skin tingling and palms sweaty as he crept to the door and peered through the slats. So possessed that he didn't realize anything was amiss about the scene…

It shouldn't have been tearing flesh. It *should* have been the slicing sound of a butcher's blade. A grunt of effort or chop of a cleaver for punctuation. Maybe the rattle of a bone and the appreciative growl of a mutt.

Varney heard nor saw any of those things as he peered through the slats.

A Terran man stood hunched over the butcher's block, the front half of a hog lying before him. He wore rags and stared at the wall in front of him with determination. He was incredibly pale, thin, with hair shorn short.

At first, Varney thought him a beggar, and his brow wrinkled at the unexpected sight, but soon Varney's eyes widened.

The man was eating—his mouth and hands were colored deep red with blood. But it was his chewing that gave the vampyre pause. His jaw was far too large as he chewed, giving the impression of a snake or a shark rather than a man. He swallowed and his throat bulged like a frog's as the meat slid down.

Then the man grasped the remaining half of the hog—far easier than a man should've been able—and took another bite.

His mouth opened, jaw stretching nearly two feet down and nearly as wide, revealing rows of dagger sharp teeth as long as Varney's hand. Instead of biting into the hog, he bit *through it,* and resumed chewing.

It was gruesome and methodical, and Varney couldn't help but watch, even as his stomach turned.

At some point in his voyeurism, Varney caught the faint scent of something sickly sweet inside the cabin, like fermenting fruit. In reflex, he swallowed and his throat clicked dryly. For a moment, fear and hunger jostled within him. He scanned the cabin, trying to find the source of the smell. It wasn't the hog—of that he was sure. But the only other option was the strange man or his saliva that strung from his mouth as he chewed…

One more bite, and the hog was gone. He chewed twice and the bones were pulverized. Only the sound of mashing flesh remained. He swallowed, throat and gut distending, and continued staring at the wall.

Sweat ran down Varney's forehead. A part of him very much wanted to attack this man—needed to. But the rest of his body was paralyzed with fear like a mouse who'd stumbled upon a cat.

"I see you, Varney Barris." His voice was warm, and might've even been comforting… but his face didn't match his tone. His face was completely blank. It reminded Varney of his father…

As a young lad—ages ago—Varney had stolen his father's knife. When the old man caught him with it… Varney's father had used the same tone with him. He knelt down and beckoned him over, face as blank as a corpse. Varney was just a boy, but even then he knew. He *knew.* Varney shuffled over to his father…

Varney didn't see his father's face change. His father clocked him in the head and sent him into the wall. Varney didn't see his father's face change at all—he was too busy clutching his head as the old man pummeled him.

Varney only knew that at some point his father started screaming at him. He didn't have to look up to imagine the sneer twisted onto his father's face as he cursed and swung.

The man in the cabin turned his head and stared at the vampyre.

The memory was pushed aside as *that stare* bored holes through Varney. Shame saddled up beside Varney's fear. The man knew he'd been watching—he'd known the whole time. He knew Varney had come hunting. He could probably smell the liquor on Varney's breath. Even knew Varney was a sham and didn't deserve *Les Enfants Terribles*. Varney's shame grew until he felt pitiful and small, like a scolded child.

And while Varney's internal crisis unfolded, the man simply stared at him through the slats as if he expected nothing less.

Finally, the man spoke again, and Varney knew that every ounce of fear and shame writhing inside him wasn't enough.

"Come here, Varney."

~ ~ ~

Chapter 1
The Return of Santa Anna

KEVRIL BERSK WALKED the surrounding gardens of the Septriones Church. The grounds stretched out into the distance, mottled with graves and peaked with spiked grave markers. Past that, hills rolled to the horizon.

Only minutes ago, he'd walked out of the church in frustration and dejection, having been barred from decisions about the return of the demons and barred from seeing Santa Anna. Now, he walked with Columen Devery, retracing his steps back toward Septriones.

Bersk was conflicted. On one hand, he couldn't wait to see the look on Leo Greghan's face when Bersk walked in with the archleon's superior having reversed all of the archleon's decries. But it would be short-lived mirth in the face of the conversation he'd just had.

The monster hunter and the columen had just spoken of the many coincidences surrounding Bersk, and the conversation swirled in the hunter's gut. Bersk had just brought news of an elder demon's rise—one who might be a member of the Desolate Family and herald the end of days. The same day, Santa Anna was brought home for questioning for her sudden and unsanctioned gallivanting to the Frozen Isles.

Kevril Bersk was apprehensive enough walking through the grounds and ground floors of Septriones, let alone with a pillar of the Church. But as the young columen said, Bersk was also at the center of these coincidences.

Taken together, Bersk would've felt more comfortable walking into a den of monsters than back into Septriones.

Columen Devery walked beside Bersk, completely unperturbed. Devery was a strapping young man, his face a healthy tan from his duties as a vassal of the Church and his smile almost naively bright. He greeted every member they passed by name, no matter their station.

Devery had a disarming sense about him. Even though the two men made a stark contrast walking beside one another, warrior and columen, Bersk was only vaguely aware of it.

"I'll do the talking," Devery said off-handedly as they walked. "Don't trifle yourself with the concerns of the living."

Bersk tried to quiet his concerns, but he couldn't help but feel apprehension as they neared the main road in front of Septriones. The Church felt more like a sepulcher than usual. It wasn't until they turned in the opposite direction of the church that Bersk let out a breath he didn't know he'd been holding.

Of course, Santa Anna would be in one of the holding cells.

Devery glanced at Bersk, but said nothing.

The columen led him to a cluster of graves marked by a single visage of an armilux—a messenger angel. It was little more than a flying eye, the width of an arm, with twenty wings stretched out from its center. The tips of the stone wings stretched up some twenty feet tall and just as wide. It was all things messenger, harbinger, and omen.

The statue sat upon a stone base—the entrance to the old sepulcher beneath. Devery walked up to the cutaway and said the old words, asking for blessing for him and for Bersk. Then he led the hunter underground.

~

Columen and hunter descended the stone stairs, passing torches kept alight by simple magic. These were remnants from an older time. There were scripts and sigils that would've worked better—would've cast the hallway in steady, even light—but the leaders of the Church were men of god, not men of change.

The light dimmed to an ominous level as they stepped into a short hall and stood before ancient stone doors.

Again, Columen Devery said a prayer for the both of them, and the doors parted. Beyond was an open room, flanked by dozens of sets of doors on either side. The whole of the room was filled with haphazardly arranged tables, chairs, and book-shelves, and conspiratorially lit with standing torches. Aside from the many books and scrolls left out, there were a dozen scrying orbs on the tables—each a twenty-pound sphere of magic glass. Each was tied to a nearby chamber so that whole gatherings could watch interrogations…

Bersk nearly winced at the thought of Santa Anna in one of those rooms. He could only hope that a saint was being treated better than he himself had been at the hands of the Church.

And yet, Bersk's heart was pounding, not from that, but from being so close to seeing her again.

The thought had flustered Bersk so much that he didn't hear the voices in the back of the room, hidden behind shelves and piles of books.

Columen Devery led the way, winding through the tables and chairs without moving a single one. As if he'd already been in and out of the room a dozen times.

A half a dozen members of the Church gathered in the back of the room, huddled around a table and spoke in hushed tones. Bersk immediately recognized his seigneur, Pater O'Malley, and the stumpy Archleon Greghan. The latter of which was speaking in wide gestures, despite his low voice. Lastly, there was the shrewd elven Archleon, Simara, no doubt an advocate for Santa Anna. Few elves sought out the Church and fewer still rose high in its ranks. Simara was noteworthy for both her wisdom and judgment, no doubt from her long life.

There were two other priests and another archleon that Bersk didn't recognize. All three seemed to recoil slightly from Greghan's gestures.

As they neared, Greghan paused his whispering tirade and glared at Bersk. Greghan drew a deep breath. "I thought I made myself clear, *former* Knight, just how I felt about your involvement—"

"Greghan," Devery said, cutting his subordinate off calmly. "Kevril Bersk is here of my volition."

Greghan glanced between the two men, and for once, another soul drew his ire more than Bersk did.

Greghan stood up as straight as he could muster, his stomach rocking the table. "Need I remind you, eminence, of the gravity of this matter. It hardly seems fitting for a wandering soul such as him to be in this room at all."

The priests in the room stared intently at the floor, while Archleon Simara's eyes widened. Even Bersk and O'Malley were taken aback. Greghan was a blowhard and an asshole, but he was no fool.

And speaking against a columen was beyond foolish.

Devery's face didn't crack or even strain. "Leo Greghan, I am in charge of this investigation, and my word is beyond reproach."

Neither did Greghan back down. He leaned both hands on the table in front of him. "Your word is received, your eminence. But the eyes of the columen and the saints are watching you. Don't forget that I have more of their ears than you do." With that, Greghan adjusted his robes as he sat, pleased with himself.

Bersk wasn't sure what he was more surprised with: Greghan's insubordination or the unfaltering stride with which Devery took it.

Devery asked, "Archleon Simara, you've spoken with Santa Anna since she's returned?"

Simara nodded, white locks of hair peeking from behind her hood. "She's cooperated fully during her apprehension and with routine questioning, but flatly refused to speak of what she found until she could do so with a columen or another saint."

Greghan huffed, but Pater O'Malley added quietly, "As is her right." No member of the Church needed answer to someone beneath them.

Columen Devery nodded to both statements. "Very well. My presence should assuage her concerns. However, I will not be the one to question her." Devery turned and nodded to Bersk, and the hunter hid his surprise as best he could.

Devery continued, "Kevril Bersk, question Santa Anna enough to corroborate her story and as much as she allows, but do not pry. This isn't her trial."

Silence hung in the room. Greghan fumed, while several others seemed frozen.

Greghan's voice came out as a hiss. "What *is* this, columen?"

"A show of good faith," Devery replied, meeting Bersk's eyes. "And a test."

Bersk nodded, but his heart was pounding. Devery's words were clear: This was as much a test for Anna as it was for Bersk. Would she cooperate with the Church? How would she handle the sudden change of terms? Could Bersk put aside his personal feelings and work for the greater good?

Worse, now Bersk held both their lives in his hands.

The irony wasn't lost on Bersk as he walked over to the holding cell. It was both the mundanity of an interrogation and the existential threat of apocalypse looming over them, and he couldn't fight his way out of it. None of Bersk's gifts or spells would be of any help.

~

Bersk walked to the stone doors that marked Santa Anna's holding cell. Behind him, Columen Devery was saying the old worlds, and when the command finished, the doors would open.

But to Bersk, the moment lingered.

How many times had he longed to see her again? Dreamed of seeing her?

Devery's words faded until they sounded as if they were a mile away.

One of Bersk's spells, *Deathbed Revelation,* could freeze time. The Gray Queen's power slowed everything, even other gods, to allow the dying a chance to repent. As the moment lingered around Bersk, he felt as if he were caught in his own spell. Like he was a man about to die.

When the doors finally opened, Bersk felt as if he were stepping into a dream.

The room was richly furnished and plush. Cushions and blankets covered the stone outcroppings that served as a long bench and bed. Reds and whites dominated the room. Santa Anna sat at a circular table in the center of the room, practicing her calligraphy. The smell of ink hung in the air, and the table was covered in paper, each sheet scrawled with runes.

Santa Anna wore a plain white robe instead of her vestments, her sleeves bunched and hair tied so neither dangled in the ink.

Her face caught Bersk off guard. He'd scarcely seen her without her hood up; he'd almost forgotten the dark curls of her hair.

Anna hadn't noticed him—hadn't so much as glanced out of the corner of her eye. Bersk had to will himself forward.

He stopped at the side of the table, attention drawn to the runes she worked carefully on. Two were infernal runes. Others were for protection. Two others matched designs he'd seen on the altar… This was more than coincidence.

Bersk was so caught up in her work that he didn't notice Anna staring up at him. The smallest hint of a smile crossed her lips.

For a long moment, neither said anything.

"Hello, Bersk," Anna finally said.

There were spells that hinged upon knowing a creature's name and using its name to control it. There were poems that claimed the opposite, that a name was merely a descriptor—that a rose was still a rose, no matter what it was called.

It was only fitting that the sellsword had hung on Anna's every word, hoping that she would call him Kev. He hoped it was just a formality.

"Santa Lucia," he replied, using the official address. *Saints of the Light.*

Her face remained stoic. "Where is Columen Devery?"

Bersk glanced back at the stone doors, which had slid shut behind him. "The columen requested that I speak to you first."

"I guessed as much. No one but Devery would go over Greghan's head and let you in here. Is the archleon keeping well?"

"As well as can be expected."

Santa Anna smirked. "I'm surprised he's still with the living. Is he boiling out there now?"

Bersk failed to suppress a smile. "No doubt listening in on this interrogation."

Anna smiled, and silence fell between them. Silence that Bersk needed to fill.

"You're not wearing your vestments."

Anna glanced down at her calligraphy before replying, "At the moment, I'm not beyond reproach." Then she turned back to him. "Why are you here, Bersk?"

"I was worried about you."

Anna seemed taken aback by his honesty, but replied, "I'm in good hands with the Church."

That time, Bersk succeeded in keeping a straight face. He cleared his throat. "Why were you in the Frozen Isles?"

For a moment, Anna seemed to consider her answer, but she sat up straight with poise. "I'll tell you everything. Everything that I've told the Church thus far. I assume you've given permission to speak to me because the Church is going to utilize you somehow… But some things will have to wait until my trial."

"Very well," Bersk replied, taking a seat on the bench.

"I was investigating demonic ruins that might have held information about Ariazi, the altars, and a prophecy."

"There's been no shortage of altars," Bersk added.

"And there will be more still. The altars are tied to the emergence of greater demons, including the Desolate Family… But you already know this, don't you, Bersk?"

He winced at the name. "I think I met one of them. Pater O'Malley and Leo Greghan are conferring with the other diocese, but… It might be Belial, the Son."

Santa Anna's mask of calm wavered. "And to think they still don't believe me…" She met Bersk's eyes with a feverish intensity. "They're going to need you," she said. "They're going to need everyone they can get."

"I know," he replied, without pomp or bravado. Knights, former or otherwise, were not tools that could be discounted. Even Greghan's doubts would be silenced.

Bersk asked, "Did you find anything that could help us?"

Anna shook her head and scoffed. "I didn't explore as deep as I hoped. The ruins weren't exactly *unguarded*, and the Church came for me…" Anna trailed off, as if she were biting her tongue.

Bersk shook his head in frustration. He had *too* many questions, and this was a right time for the Church to muck things up. What lead did Anna have that pointed to the Frozen Isles and those ruins in particular? Why had the Church decided to apprehend her when so many other diocese pursued flagrant interests—

The stone doors of Anna's cell slid open and the observation group barged in, led by Leo Greghan. He was fuming.

Greghan said, "You know damn well why you were brought back—"

Moving quickly, Columen Devery grabbed the archleon by the shoulder. *"That is enough,* Greghan," Devery said curtly. It was the first time Bersk had seen his calm demeanor waver, but his words did their part. The room was thoroughly silenced.

Only then did Devery continue. "The elders have their reasons, Santa Anna. These are trying times, and the only way that we shall see through them is with unity of will." Devery turned to Bersk. "Kevril Bersk, you will return to Ozequn and then report to the Church of Arkcaster. I've already sent orders that the Order is to use you however they see fit."

Bersk nodded as the finality of the decree set in. Santa Anna's trial would start soon, and Bersk would be half a world away with his own problems to contend with.

But once again, Bersk felt as if time had slowed—as if he were under the effects of the *Deathbed Revelation* spell. As if the world was waiting for him to repent—to say *something*. But under his goddess's spell, the dying ever only got one confession—no matter the life they had lived.

What was Bersk supposed to say?

His eyes fell on the bare stone walls as he muttered his goodbyes. "Diocese… Santa Lucia…" Bersk left without meeting her eyes.

"Goodbye, Bersk," she replied.

The stone doors slid shut behind him, and Bersk walked past the remaining diocese. His steps only sped up as he climbed the stairs until he emerged in the open air.

Caught between a Church he could not leave, a goddess he couldn't deny, and a saint he couldn't have.

~

Bersk stood in the cluster of graves, breathing deep. The statue of the armilux angel stood behind him, a frozen watcher.

Bersk tried to collect himself. He had more important things than to worry about a saint who could take care of herself.

But he couldn't shake one thing she had said—that she was in *good hands* with the Church. It wasn't the kind of thing that would've tipped off the diocese listening in to their conversation, but it was unmistakably a code that Bersk would understand:

Someone in the Church was working against Santa Anna. Someone meant to stop her from finding *something* at the ruins of the Mecendu.

It meant that someone either had a vendetta against Anna, or, more pressingly, that someone in the Church had been corrupted and is helping the demons.

Footsteps sounded behind him, and Bersk whirled around, far more startled and more eager than he should've been.

Pater O'Malley stood at the sepulcher entrance, looking as surprised as Bersk was. O'Malley asked, "Were you expecting someone else?"

"No," Bersk replied, unconvincingly.

O'Malley's face softened and he looked up at the sky. Bersk wondered if he was debating whether to comment on his protege or if he really missed seeing the clouds that much.

In the end, his seigneur said neither.

"The Church is taking the matter of the Desolate Family seriously. They're mobilizing the Order of Kripishi in cities across Ozequn."

"Good."

"Devery asked me to send word of your arrival to the head of the Order in Arkcaster," O'Malley said. "...I haven't told them yet."

Bersk sighed and nodded. "Thank you for that. I'd rather look around the city first, before getting ordered around."

"I suspected as much, but Bersk, don't dawdle. I wouldn't be surprised if Greghan has his own channels to keep tabs on you. Lord knows the man has spite enough for you and Santa Anna."

"Greghan is the least of my worries."

"Regardless... Keep your wits about you, Bersk. There's—there's a chance I'm wrong about the Son."

Bersk scoffed. "You're never wrong."

But O'Malley's demeanor only grew more serious. "Some of the accounts say that the Bastard is the first to rise—not the Son. If that's the case... you might not be fighting a skirmish against some demons and a few vampyre. You'll be fighting a war against an entire city."

Bersk knew enough of the prophecies. Belial, the son of Ariazi, may have been a general of the damned, but it was a fight that Bersk and the Knights of Kripishi were suited for—after all, they were hunters of monsters and demons, alike.

But the Bastard… he was a manipulator of Terrans. He could command elves and men as easily as his brethren commanded demons.

A long moment passed, and Bersk said quietly, "There's something else. There might be a mole in the Church. Someone working against Santa Anna and possibly against us."

Pater O'Malley glanced to the sepulcher and back to Bersk, as if asking if Anna had confided this in him. Bersk nodded.

The priest rubbed his temples. "The scriptures talk of *festering wounds*… Maybe Santa Anna is right. I'll keep it quiet, for now, but eventually I'll have to go to the diocese."

What O'Malley left unspoken was: *Even if one of the dioceses is the mole.*

Bersk replied, "Keep your wits about you." Then he thumbed the face of his lodestone. *"Ad locum meum."*

~ ~

ARCHLEON GREGHAN LEANED against the back wall of the holding cell, trying to let the cold stone on his back take his mind off his *absolute irritation*.

"When will my trial start?" Santa Anna asked the columen. All things considered, she looked like she was taking her current predicament well.

Too well.

Archleon Greghan watched them both carefully.

"Your first hearings will be in two days' time," Columen Devery said, hands clasped in front of him. "In the meantime, we'll not disturb you unless necessary."

The saint nodded to Devery without sparing so much as a glance in Greghan's direction.

No matter. There was nothing that would save her now. Greghan felt a smug sense of satisfaction at the thought, though he kept his expression as blank as he could.

When one acted outside the arms and protection of the Church, there should be consequences. And when the natural consequences did not arrive fast enough, the law should speed them along.

The insolent woman had been hanging around with Kevril Bersk too long, and his misguided ideals had rubbed off on her.

No one was above the laws of the Church.

Not Kevril Bersk.

Not Santa Anna.

Columen Devery turned to leave, and Archleon Greghan cast his eyes downward, lest the young man see the glimmer in his eye.

Not even Columen Devery was above the law, and Greghan couldn't wait until the young columen reaped his choices in this sepulcher.

Greghan followed Devery out of the cell and spared no more thought or a glance backward as the stone doors shut.

They had work to do.

~ ~ ~

Chapter 2
The City of Arkcaster

BERSK REAPPEARED ON the other side of the world.

The lodestone worked quickly and silently, without even the sensation of movement or vertigo. One moment he was at Septriones Church, the next he was back on the continent of Ozequn.

The sun was already sagging in the sky and the wind was already cool. It would be a cold night.

He stood at the top of a crater, looking down at the destruction the demon had wrought. A tangled mass of stone pillars protruded from the center—the remnants of the demon's spell. Threaded between the stone were the remnants of the Formicae queen's corpse. Dozens of ravens and crows adorned the corpse, squawking and peeling away the flesh.

Only one raven sat atop the stone pillars, unmoved by the feast below.

Archimedes flew over to the hunter and landed on his shoulder. Bersk rubbed his feathers and the psychopomp cooed in greeting.

"I missed you too, old friend," Bersk replied.

~

Kevril Bersk started running.

Tamren Jorbough was marching to the city of Arkcaster with the military brigade led by Captain Henring. They were at least a half day ahead of Bersk, and though Tam would be safe with them, Bersk didn't intend to travel behind his friend for long.

So, with Archimedes flying ahead, Bersk ran through most of the night and the following day, stopping only for three hours to sleep. His spell of strength helped and Bersk could have run longer, but it wasn't good to push the body so long and so hard with magic—

Not when he had farther to travel to Arkcaster and he had an elder demon to hunt.

~

Bersk caught up to Tam and Captain Henring's brigade the following night, damn near giving the lookouts a heart attack.

It seemed as if the rumors had made their rounds of the demon heading for home—all the men were on edge, including Tam and the Captain.

Bersk mentioned pertinent details of his conversation in Septriones with Captain Henring—which was to say, minimal. Henring seemed at least a little relieved to see Bersk and that he would be joining with the Knights in Arkcaster to hunt the demon.

Afterward, Bersk pulled Tam to the edge of camp and gave him the full story. Even though there were no more vampyres or anyone else with enhanced hearing left in the brigade, Bersk still waited until they had a moment alone to speak at length. And even though there were no more predators around, Tam was still hesitant standing so far from the campfire.

Tam stroked his beard, chuckling with gallows humor as his eyes scanned the darkness. "Back into the dragon's maw, then? Can't say I'm not surprised."

Bersk patted him on the shoulder. "Did you think that the Knights of Kripishi would have it all sorted out before we got there?"

"Not anymore," the bard replied with a grin. "Well, come on. I wasn't trying to live forever, anyway."

~

They marched double time back to Arkcaster. Even with frequent breaks, it was a brutal pace for the soldiers. But none complained. All seemed aware of the gravity of the situation.

Tam was a different story. Without Bersk's magic, the bard wouldn't have been able to keep such a pace. Tam was able to keep up with the bolstered strength spell, but by the final hours, Bersk's mind felt numb from concentrating on it.

~

It wasn't until the final night, camped under the stars, that Tam asked Bersk about Anna. The pair lay side by side on bedrolls, sharing a long blanket turned sideways. A cloudless night sky hung overhead.

Tam asked, "How was she?" Since Bersk had returned, both men had been careful not to refer to Anna by title.

Bersk stifled a laugh. "Now you ask me? We're less than a day from Arkcaster and *now* you ask me?"

Tam waved a dismissive hand. "I'm not one to pry, but it seemed like it weighed on you when you returned."

"Could've been the demon."

"Come now, Bersk. When have you ever been so broken up over a demon?"

Bersk wordlessly conceded the point and silence fell between the men.

"I'm just saying… It's not a good look for you, Bersk."

The hunter nodded.

Tam sighed and stretched his legs. "Well, when you do want to talk about her, just let me know. I've found it's better to air one's thoughts on women, lest they maintain a hold over you."

"I was doing fine until you mentioned her."

Tam scoffed and laid his hat over his face. "I'm sure you were, old boy."

Bersk closed his eyes. He had been doing fine—he *usually* was, so long as he had something to focus on. It was these quiet moments where there was nothing else to do that he couldn't help his mind from wandering.

A large part of Bersk was anxious to get to Arkcaster, if only so hunting a demon could take his mind off of other things.

~

The brigade saw Arkcaster at the end of the second day.

They crossed through some miles of farm fields and hamlets that surrounded the city. From atop the hills, they could see almost the entire length of it; Arkcaster was long and thin, flanking both sides of the Vallams river for over a mile. Three drawbridges spanned the width of the Vallams and were lit by blue-green flames that burned bright even in the early hours of the evening. Bersk suspected the bridge was laden with scripts and runes; these would draw power from the river similar to a water wheel and result in constant power so long as the river kept flowing. A half dozen masts from docked ships peeked over the buildings.

It was the elves that taught men those tricks. Elves fled their homeland and brought knowledge of how to siphon latent environmental power with runes. The elven city of Novissimé supposedly had towers that reached up to the sky, torches that burned forever, running water, and self-cleansing sewers.

As the brigade marched the final road to Arkcaster, the sun fell low, and the blue-green flames of the bridges seemed to spread out across the city, casting the lot of it in ethereal glow. It was a beautiful and powerful sight—magic that man was only beginning to harness. Perhaps the humans had learned something from the elves after all.

They passed a handful of farmers returning with unsold produce and no other travelers. The sun was nearly set by the time they made it to the city gate proper—the sky bleeding red while the city glowed below. Captain Henring saluted the guards at the main gate, and he ushered Bersk and Tam through with his men.

The guards jeered some of the soldiers as they passed—friends, Bersk suspected—but the soldiers returned only half-hearted greetings.

Inside the city walls, Arkcaster was a mix of beauty and stench. There were two main streets—one on either side of the river, and each running parallel with it. Like most cities, these were paved, and during the day they would be lined with store-fronts, carts, and all manner of artisans hawking their wares. But the side streets were unpaved, full of mud and muck. Horse manure was swept clean from the streets most nights, but the runoff from pisspots never left the side streets—except for particularly heavy downpours.

Kevril Bersk and Tamren Jorbough followed the brigade down the main street. Archimedes flew from rooftop to roof-top, keeping an eye on Bersk and the surrounding street.

Though the workday was done, night stretched on in the city. A half dozen taverns and nearly as many brothels opened along the cobbles, beckoning in the weary, promising relief in all manners in exchange for their hard-earned coin of the day. Thin poles flanked the sides of the street, nearly as tall as the buildings, and each topped with a blue-green flame. Bersk leaned close to one pole as he passed and nodded with satis-faction as he saw a string of script wrapping up the length of it.

His satisfaction was short-lived, however. Bersk remem-bered why he loathed cities. It wasn't just the smell or the crowded streets and hovels packed with people. It wasn't even the desperate *need* of those people—for money, food, sex, or liquor.

It was all of it.

Cities were too much stimulation for Bersk. Too much to focus on and to parse.

Hunting was simple. People, even, were simple. But cities, bureaucracy… it was all *too much* for Bersk.

"Bersk, are you alright?" Tam asked.

Bersk blinked and forced himself to snap out of it. "I'm fine. It's just been a while."

Tam chuckled uneasily. "Good thing I'm here with you. Otherwise you'll wind up like those poor sods." Tam gestured to two men outside the next tavern. They spoke nervously, and more than once both glanced at the brigade of soldiers.

As Bersk looked around, he found that others were watching them and the brigade with curious eyes. Some even looked hopeful—as if the sight of soldiers in the evening was a good thing.

"I think we're behind schedule," Bersk muttered.

"You saw that too?" Tam asked. "Glad it wasn't just me. Folks are skittish tonight."

As they walked, Bersk noticed more and more eyes flitting nervously around. Some looked to the brigade, but more seemed to watch the alleys where the eerie light of the torches didn't reach.

~

The Arkcaster barracks were in the center of town, a squat, nondescript square of bricks and steel. As they approached, Captain Henring called for the soldiers to disperse.

Henring turned to Bersk, the grizzled captain looking weary enough to sleep standing up. "The Church is on the other side of the Vallams. Praetor Farglory is in charge. She'll want to see you."

"Sleep first," Bersk replied.

"We can put you up in the barracks," Henring offered.

The offer caught Bersk off guard. Either the Captain was feeling particularly thankful, or Bersk had made his resignation from the Order of Kripishi too well known.

"An inn is fine," Bersk replied, but nodded in thanks.

"Be seeing you, Bersk," Henring said, and followed his men into the barracks.

Kevril Bersk and Tam tried three inns before they finally found one with vacancies. Three merchant ships were harbored on the river and had brought travelers as well as fresh transport from the South.

They stood in the small opening of the Blue Mermaid Inn, Bersk eyeing the tasteful mascot statue while the elven innkeeper went on about the fresh fruit from the ships.

Despite his weariness, Tam perked up at the mention of them, then immediately expressed disbelief when Bersk replied that he'd never had them.

"Haven't you been there when you fought…" Tam trailed off, then shook his head and whispered to the innkeeper. "Man lives in the jungle for a few months and never thinks to try the fruit."

Bersk was so tired, all he could do was chuckle.

Traveling and having time for indulgence were two different things, after all.

~

The next morning, hunter and bard woke groggily at first light, ate downstairs, then walked to the docks.

Bersk led them down the main street and toward the middle bridge of the city. Despite the early morning hours, they were already skirting wagons and carts full of produce from the fields surrounding Arkcaster.

Archimedes followed from the rooftops, and Bersk could feel a tinge of annoyance from the raven at being left outside overnight.

Bersk glanced up to the roofs and muttered, "Sorry, old friend."

"What's the plan?" Tam asked, adjusting the frills of his shirt.

"Last time I was here, there was an old hunter named Willem. He'd… retired, and taken to working the docks." Bersk hadn't meant to draw Tam's attention to the fact, but he could already feel the bard's eyes on him. So Bersk added, "Vampyre blood."

"You mean he was attacked?"

"No," Bersk replied. He paused at the bridge and looked out over the Vallams. He could see clear down the length of the river—all three bridges, each with a small port and ship docked at it.

Bersk continued, "Hunters will take any edge we can get—weapons, potions, artifacts… Willem drank vampyre blood. It's very potent, but it has *side effects*."

"You have a talent for the ominous," Tam replied. "And you suppose our man is down there?"

Bersk nodded, then led the way down the wooden planks. Archimedes let out a long call and watched.

They found Willem at the Northern dock. He was a hunched, wiry man when Bersk first met him, and now Willem was even more so. The former hunter and a young man were each carrying one half of a crate. After they set it down, the lad gestured over to Bersk and Tam. Willem met Bersk's eyes—

For a moment, Bersk worried Willem didn't recognize him.

"You're a long way from Pritaveru," Bersk called.

Willem nodded slightly, then waved the young man away. He half-walked, half-hobbled over to Bersk.

"That's one I haven't heard in a while," Willem said, glancing up at both Bersk and Tam. The former hunter was so hunched that he scarcely came up to Bersk's chest.

"You have a lot of connections these days?" Bersk asked.

"You're not my betrothed, Mr. Bersk. I speak to as many people as I like. Come on," Willem said with a wave. "I'm due for my break."

Willem led them over to an empty section of the docks. He shuffled close to the wall and beneath the shade before removing his cap and running a hand through his hair. Willem still kept it long, but it had thinned even more than when Bersk last saw him.

That was the curse of vampyre blood. Using it made a hunter stronger, for a time. Use it too often, and it warped both the body and the lifespan.

Willem held the cap nervously in both hands. "What brings you to beautiful Arkcaster?"

"Nothing fun," Bersk replied. "I need to find the dens."

Bersk watched Willem out of the corner of his eye, trying to gauge the man's reaction.

"Hunting monsters used to be fun… for some of us, anyway," the old hunter muttered. He was biding his time, trying to gauge Bersk as much as he was.

"You here for them?" Willem finally asked.

"No, I'm not here for them," Bersk replied, "but I do need to talk to them."

Willem nodded and a relief settled into the creases of his face. "That's good. Arkcaster and the dens have a good thing going. Would hate for someone like you to muck it up."

"I hunt monsters, and only monsters."

Willem waved him off. "Lord and I know, Mr. Bersk. That's the only reason I'm telling you."

Bersk waited while the former hunter mulled something over.

In the end, his patience got the better of him.

"You still haven't told me where I can find them," Bersk said.

Willem nodded, and after another moment, leaned forward and whispered, "Go to the shops on Westmissen. *Les Enfants Terribles* is the name. There's a door 'round back, looks like it's been burned and might crumble to ash."

"Wards…"

"Yeah. Walk up to that door intending to talk to them and it will let you pass. Walk up with any other intentions and you won't find it, no matter how hard you look. Anyway, tell them I sent you. Ask for Varnay Barris. He's new management, trying to make a name for himself. He works with all types."

Bersk chuckled.

Willem looked up at him and narrowed his eyes. "Look, Bersk. Don't muck this up. Please."

Berks's reflex had been to joke. It seemed like a lot of hunters found humor in danger and darkness—it had certainly been that way last time Bersk had seen Willem. But now, Bersk saw nothing but pleading in the old man's eyes, raw like an open wound.

"I give you my word," Bersk replied, knowing that a hunter would be satisfied with little else.

Willem merely turned and walked back across the docks, all too eagerly.

Tam piped up from beside him. "What was all that about?" Bersk had nearly forgotten Tam was there.

"He's using again."

"You think he's hunting again, too?"

Bersk shook his head. "No. He's just trying to maintain. That's why he was worried about the den. Probably has a deal with one of the residents. Come on. Let's go."

Thankfully, Tam dropped the subject.

It was hard enough to survive being a hunter just to die a slow death as a man.

~ ~ ~

Chapter 3
Le Enfant Terrible

WHEN THE ELVES began their slow withdrawal from the world, other Terran civilizations expanded to fill the gaps. Humans were the most prolific, and some would say that their society has dwarfed even the heights of the ancient elves.

But there were many creatures that lived in the shadows of Terran civilization.

There were some, like werewolves and wendigos, that were merely sparse curses. Mermaids, sprites, and fey were wanderers from other planes, some of which lost the ability to return to their native realms. And of course there were full-fledged demons and the many demon-blooded that crossed over.

Of all the demon-blooded, other-planar, and non-standard Terrans, only vampyres could boast about having a complete society hidden away. They were one of the oldest and shrewd-est demon-blooded races. Over time, their kind had infiltrated every city big enough to support their hunger.

Twice there had been open war: Once between elves and vampyres, and again between humans and vampyres. The elves were the original aggressors and stopped short when they suffered too many casualties. The second, most recent war, the vampyres had been the aggressors, and found themselves in much the same predicament.

Kevril Bersk and Tamren Jorbough walked the cobbles of the main street, idly following the crowd.

Bersk was telling Tam about the history of the vampyres—as much as the bard might need to understand the situation.

Bersk walked and narrated, paying just enough attention to himself, while the rest of his attention was looking through the eyes of Archimedes. The raven hopped from rooftop to rooftop while watching the crowd around Bersk and Tam.

From up top, the street looked little different from the bubbling Vallams river, albeit a little more colorful between the clothes and the fruit wagons.

So far, no one was following them. Which was good, because Bersk didn't want to unknowingly bring an enemy to a vampyre blood den.

"You see," Bersk continued, "Vampyres realized they didn't want to rule. It was much easier to stay in the shadows. To live in secret and subtly influence human civilization only when needed."

Tam walked beside him, hands clasped behind his back, and listening intently. "And how do you know all this?"

"The Church maintains information on *all Terrans*, not just their capabilities and weaknesses, but as detailed histories of the species as they can."

Tam nodded along. "And you're still content to go to this den tonight? Why not go now?"

"How polite would you be if I knocked on your door while you were sleeping?"

"Point taken. Do you think we'll run into Xandra and Weylan?" The bard shivered as he mentioned Sergeant Weylan.

The pair of vampyres had been hiding their secret and serving as upper ranks of the Arkcaster military. Their brigade had stumbled upon the Formicae hive that summoned their current demon problem, and the pair had personally aided Bersk and Tam in destroying the altar.

But now their truth had been revealed, and Xandra and Weylan were on the run. There was a chance that the pair would flee the city, but Bersk was betting they were lying low inside Arkcaster.

"This isn't the only den in the city, but I'm hoping we do run into them," Bersk admitted. "Their recounting of events could give us credit with the den."

"Right, right. Unless the demon gets to them first… and turns them against us."

Bersk pulled his attention from Archimedes and glanced sidelong at the bard. "That's not your usual optimistic self."

Tam shrugged. "These are dark times." He'd said the line sarcastically, but not even the bard's levity could lessen the truth.

~

They waited until sunset to go to the den. Blue-green light flickered over the streets as Bersk and Tam walked.

Two shops sat on the corner of Westmissen and First—a tailor and a cobbler, complete with a boy standing out front and hawking for both stores. He might've been twelve or thirteen, his freckled face red with exertion, but he stopped yelling only to take a breath.

"You, sir!" the boy hollered to Tam. "You're a man who knows his dress. You should stop in for a new vest or a petticoat."

Bersk stopped only when Tam did.

Tam stood beside the lad, looking down at him expectantly. "Do you know their wares?" The boy nodded. "Do they have Sireel cotton and Tenthrian silk?"

"Plenty of that cotton, sir, but the silk is hard to come by, so the tailor makes each piece to order."

Tam smiled at that, then asked, "Have you been out here all day, son?"

"Yes, sir."

The bard nodded. "I'll tell the master that he owes you a cut of my purchase."

They walked down the side street, while the lad hollered thanks to Tam.

Tam noticed Bersk's side eye and replied, "Hard work and good taste should be rewarded."

Bersk chuckled, "Say no more."

They turned into the small alley that led behind the shops—the passage so thin that they had to walk single file.

True to Willem's word, there was a charred door tucked away at the end of the alley. The planks of it were viciously pitted and crusted with gray ash, as if it had been recently set alight.

Above, Archimedes crowed in annoyance.

"Sorry," Bersk replied to the psychopomp, "but I can't take you with me."

Tam cleared his throat. "Say, what's the name mean, anyway?"

Les Enfants Terribles. "Vampires are demon-blooded. They're paying homage to their legacy. It means, *the terrible children.*"

There was irony too—after all, vampyres were some of the most well-behaved of their brethren.

Bersk gripped the doorknob with his unmarred hand and felt the knob grow hot—nearly hot enough to burn. He didn't let go, and trusted his intentions to lessen the wards. He pulled the door open and the heat lessened.

Beyond was a rough stone staircase leading down into darkness. It reminded him of a tomb, except that this was far, far stranger.

"My word," Tam muttered.

Bersk walked down the stairs, and Tam hurried behind.

"Do you remember that sanctuary blessing?" Bersk asked over his shoulder.

"The one I learned from that shaman—what was his name... Yes, of course I know it. I won't be much good to you, though."

"Not for me. For you."

Tam gulped.

Darkness swallowed them on all sides, and it looked as if the stairs hung perilously above an abyss. Only the stone immediately surrounding them was lit, though there was no torch.

Bersk knew from experience that no fire or magic would push aside that darkness.

They descended almost a hundred steps. The air grew frigid.

"Bersk, how far down…"

"We should be near the end."

A moment later, the stairs ended at a stone wall and another charred door. Darkness had cloaked the steps behind them and there was no way of telling how far the stone way extended out into the black.

"This isn't real… is it?" Tam asked, eyes flitting around.

"It's a pocket realm, of sorts. We're still beneath Arkcaster, and yet, we're also a realm apart." Bersk laid a reassuring hand on his friend's shoulder. "Stick with me."

Bersk opened the door, again feeling the scalding heat of the knob give way as it opened.

For a moment, it felt as if darkness had poured out from the door, swallowing them. But in the same breath, the magic holding this place together measured them and found their intentions worthy.

Darkness receded, revealing the blood den beyond.

Once it might've been a sepulcher. Much of the stone of walls and floor were worn smooth. Alcoves lined the walls—where sarcophagi might've lain.

Now, the whole of it was richly furnished and filled with lounging vampyres instead of corpses. They sat at tables sipping mixtures of blood and alcohol, and lay on reclining beds that surrounded the room. The furniture was all a mix of dark wood and plush cushion. Everlit candles cast the room in a dim light and magic fountains bubbled around the room. The latter were merely colored to give the appearance of blood and made to bubble and drip perpetually from the ceiling. Real blood would've been wasteful and prone to congealing.

It had been some time since Bersk had set foot in a blood den, and yet with all long-lived creatures, little changed in the span of a few years. Vampyre tastes were *uniform*, if anything.

In the back of the den, there was a large, high-standing table, likely one reserved for visiting masters and nobles. One vampyre sat there, alone. They wore a deep black robe that shimmered in the candlelight. Their face was hidden behind a wrap that hid everything except for piercing red eyes.

It didn't take long for the majority of the residents to notice Bersk and Tam.

Two vampyres rose from a nearby table and sauntered over. They were both dressed like nobles instead of guards, and didn't bother to conceal their wine-stained fangs.

The woman stepped in front, hands on her hips, and looked Bersk up and down. At once she might've been a farmer or laborer; her skin still looked sun-beaten with wrinkles and her shoulders were broad, but she had clearly lived long as a vampire. Her skin was as pale as any.

"You've got nerve or purpose," she said. "Not often a hunter visits here." She paid Tam no mind at all.

Even though she spoke reasonably, there was no doubt the whole den heard her. Bersk felt all the eyes in the room settle on them.

"Purpose," Bersk replied, pulling back his coat to show that he didn't have a sword…

Though his sword, *Twitch,* was never far.

Bersk continued, "Willem pointed us your way. Is the master in?"

A smirk crossed her face, and was gone just as quickly. "He's indisposed. You can speak to me."

Beside her, the young man spoke up. "You can't be serious. Varney will have our heads, speaking to a hunter—"

She glanced in the young vampyre's direction and her eyes alone were enough to still him.

"Run along," she muttered. "You two, sit with me."

The young vampyre did as he was told, and Bersk felt his eyes on them from across the room as the three sat together. Bersk sat with his back to the stone.

"My name is Dela," she said, refilling her goblet with what was left of the other vampyre's drink. She swirled it, for the first time taking in the sight of Tam. "Now, what brings you two here?"

Bersk gave their names and quickly explained what had happened on the cliffs, glossing over all but the most necessary details. "An elder demon sprang from the altar, and it was on its way here, to Arkcaster. It's likely already here."

Then he paused to see how Dela reacted. So far she'd nodded along, pausing only to swirl and sip at her drink.

"If Willem trusts you, then I'll trust you. Likely the others will too. But why come to us at all?" Dela asked, curiosity in her voice instead of accusation. "Why not go to the Church?"

Bersk tried not to meet the eyes of the other vampyres in the den—all of which were watching and listening.

"The Church already knows, but they do not know that I'm coming here."

That was what they really wanted to know, after all—that Bersk wasn't bringing the Church down upon them. A few vampyres turned back to their drinks, but not many.

"You're not with the Church?" Dela asked. Bersk shook his head. "You're freelance then? They must be paying you handsomely to come down here…" Dela's words hung in the air, accusation and fear mixed in them.

"Are you well-versed in scripture?"

"The parts that matter to us."

Bersk said, "What do you know of the Desolate Family?"

Once again, all eyes of the den were fixed on Bersk—a mix of wide eyes and uneasy laughter.

Dela kept her composure, but her hand trembled as she downed the rest of her drink. "The Church think the elder demon is one of the Desolate?"

Bersk nodded. "Maybe the Son or the Bastard, but they don't know for certain."

"It makes sense now," Dela said, nodding along. "We'll send word to the masters…" Then she chuckled grimly. "What's one more apocalypse?"

Bersk and Tam bid Dela goodbye and left.

There was nothing else to discuss. Bersk had gone to the den in part to warn the vampyres, but he had hoped they had information that could help. If they were truly blindsided by a demon in the city, then there was nothing they could offer Bersk–yet.

Bersk and Tam made their way out of the den. Bersk contemplated their next move, and spared a glance back as the door shut behind them.

All the vampyres had gone back to their drinks–save the black-clad elder in the back of the room. They were still staring at Bersk.

~

Tam ushered them quickly up the steps, through the alley, and back out into the main street of Arkcaster. The bard shivered in the blue-green light.

"I never thought I'd long for the deadly tunnels of those insects again," Tam muttered. "At least I can tell which of them wanted to eat me."

"Of all the *things* we could be looking to for help, they're the most civilized."

Tam glanced back toward the alleys and shivered again. "I won't be able to sleep a wink tonight."

Bersk looked up at the night sky, which was all but starless when seen from inside the city. Light from magic torches tended to overpower the little light that reached from the heavens; there was irony in there, Bersk was sure of it.

They walked the cobblestone street back to Blue Mermaid Inn and went back to their room on the second floor.

Bersk unlocked the door and opened it to find a pair of red eyes staring back at him from across the room.

The elder vampyre had followed them back from the den. Beside it, the window swung open on a breeze.

Tam had been in the middle of a yawn that cut off abruptly.

Bersk stared back from the doorway, right hand ready to summon *Twitch*. In a breath, he took stock of his options. The hall seemed to close in around him. Bersk had no desire to fight an elder vampire, but he would.

"Come in, please," the vampyre said, the woman's voice and her accent catching Bersk off guard.

"That's quite the trick," Bersk whispered. "Breaking into a second-story window without anyone noticing."

Some vampyre elders could shapeshift into bats or even into clouds of mist. If the elder in front of him was a mist-walker, then Bersk and Tam were in serious trouble.

"Come in, please," she repeated. "I will not violate over ten years of peace."

There was an earnesty in her voice that cut through Bersk as surely as if she'd used a blade. Slowly, Bersk and Tam stepped inside and closed the door.

Slowly, the vampyre pulled away her face covering and hood to reveal pale skin and hair even redder than her eyes.

"I have a job for you, Kevril Bersk. You can sit. I won't bite." When Bersk didn't reply, she added, "Are you a monster hunter or not?"

Bersk looked to Tam, but the bard shook his head quickly. Tam stayed by the door. Bersk walked forward and slid a chair over so that he was sitting between the vampyre and his friend.

"I'm a hunter," Bersk replied, as much to steady himself as to answer the question. Despite her assurances, Bersk was uneasy and didn't take his eyes off of her.

Bersk *was a hunter*, but his jobs didn't always end in death. Sometimes, he aided the monster or helped them escape. When both Terran and monster could be spared, Bersk tried to save both. But the truth still stood–

Monsters never came to him for help.

"So what can I help you with…"

"Lorith," she replied. "And I need you to find my brother's killer."

~ ~ ~

Chapter 4
A Lead

"HIS NAME WAS Jeremy," she said quietly. "Jeremy Barton."

Bersk nodded. Tam lit candles on the table while hunter and vampyre talked about a job.

Bersk asked, "When did he go missing?"

"Three days ago. At first, I thought he'd left… That wasn't strange for him. I never knew when I would see him or when he would disappear for weeks at a time. He loathed responsibility, you see." Lorith pulled out a bright red handkerchief and dabbed her eyes.

"He was turned too? Why not ask the dens for help?"

Lorith reached into her robe and pulled a silver necklace over her head. At the end of it hung a ruby, small and deep red. Bersk recognized the significance.

She tossed it to him and Bersk caught it in with his left hand. It had glowed brightly from across the room, but as Bersk held it, the shine seemed to fade before his eyes.

"Do you know what that is, Kevril Bersk?"

He nodded. "It's a Blood Promise. An heirloom given by family and worn by the turned." An *old* tradition, one few besides elders partook in. Lorith would know the blood of her family.

"It was returned to the den two nights ago… Returned by a young vampyre who found it in the *gutter*… I'm just thankful it was found by one of our kind and not by a human.

"My brother never left Arkcaster."

Bersk nodded, already working on theories, but he needed more.

"Again, why not go to the dens?"

"He's not the only one that's gone missing. *Les Enfants Terribles'* benefactor disappeared only a few days before. Neither could be traced. Some suspect war is brewing between the clans, but after hearing your concerns about demons…"

Lorith's cheeks were wet with tears and she didn't bother to wipe them. "There are few creatures that can kill us, Kevril Bersk. Even then, I should be able to find my brother's body. No force in the realm should be able to hide him from me."

Beside him, Tam sighed wearily. "It's already here, isn't it, Bersk?"

Lorith was right. There were few creatures capable of killing an elder vampyre and *disposing* of its body. Fewer still that could stay hidden in a city like Arkcaster.

Bersk's theories narrowed to a single one: The elder demon—the Son or the Bastard.

Bersk asked, "Do the other clans know?"

"That's what scares me most," she replied. "Outwardly, some of the clans have pointed fingers, but they're not searching for the truth. I suspect they know there's a demon among us."

That was the real reason Lorith had come to him. She suspected the masters among her kind were either complacent or—worse—already in the demon's thrall.

Which meant that things were already worse than Bersk thought.

He pocketed the ruby necklace, not waiting for Lorith's approval. If there was any hope of finding a trail, he would need it. Lorith understood.

"Where does your brother's trail end?"

~

Lorith faded into mist, and left Bersk and Tam sitting in the shadows of the room.

When she was gone, Tam walked over, closed the window and latched it. He glanced out the window suspiciously. "Did you know she could do that?"

"I had my suspicions," Bersk said as he stood and stretched. "I'm going to check out her brother's last whereabouts."

"Right now?"

"We'll have to wait to go to the Church until tomorrow morning. I'd rather go check this out now rather then when there's people walking about in the middle of the day. Are you coming?"

Tam glanced between the door and the window, weighing his options.

Bersk nearly told him that a latched window wouldn't stop an elder vampyre from getting in, but Tam answered.

"Godsdamnit."

~

Bersk and Tam slipped through the shadows. Archimedes charted their path through the winding alleys, helping the pair avoid the few guards that patrolled on night shift. With the psychopomp watching over them, it was all too easy.

They ended on the East side of Arkcaster, in the midst of poorly erected shacks that wrapped around bars and butcher's shops.

Bersk's heart swelled with pity as he ignored the sounds of drunkards and occasional weeping and the stench of languishing chamber pots.

There were problems in the world that couldn't be solved with a blade. And the people in the shanties had neither the money nor the means to solve them. Neither did Bersk.

Tam had been mostly quiet as they walked, but walked close behind Bersk now. "Why didn't she just speak to us at the den? Why the ominous visit, do you think?"

"She couldn't be seen with us," Bersk replied. Vampyres lived by their status. If Lorith was a master, then she couldn't be seen with them.

Tam started to ask something else, but Bersk waved a hand for silence. With Archimedes watching for danger from the roofs and Bersk searching the alleys for signs of struggle, the hunter's attention was split enough ways already.

Lorith only knew where her brother's necklace was found. She didn't know where he died.

Fortunately, Bersk had ways of tracking him.

Bersk paused at the alley where the necklace had been found.

"Omni-videns ordinem."

The power of the Gray Queen flowed through Bersk, and his eyes were blotted out with the same otherworldly blue as his sword. The world took on a blue tinge even more vivid than the torches from main street. Glowing tears of magic dripped from his eyes. The spell of *all-seeing order.*

He pulled the Blood Promise from his pocket and held it in front of him. As he spoke, the ruby churned with a deep purple light.

"By frozen warmth and captured dream, reveal to us thy hidden scheme. Show where thou bled, and thine path we shall redeem." The *spell of secrets*—one of the Church's most guarded magics.

Alone, neither spell would've aided Bersk, but together their powers allowed him to see into the recent past.

As the ruby glowed in his hand, he saw the ghostly image of it appear again—laying in the gutter of the alley. A single red light rose from it up into the sky.

Not into the sky—over the rooftops.

With Archimedes help, Bersk followed the red trail as it arched over two blocks and led to another alleyway.

They turned a corner, and Bersk stopped.

The alley looked innocent enough and not altogether different from any other in the dark corners of the city: The ground was muddy, scuffed and rutted from boots and wheelbarrows. Muck and mud churned together. The ramshackle walls that lined the alley looked as if they might collapse at any moment.

Even though days had passed and the scene was tainted, the truth was written in blue and red.

Lorith's brother, Jeremy, had fought for his life in this very spot. Fought and died.

The entire alleyway was stained red, as if a wave of blood had passed through. The red arc of the necklace ended in the center of the scene. Boards were busted or showed traces of fingernail gouges. Beneath the footsteps of normal the mud was pushed up against walls and odd troughs lay at the edges.

The two spells helped Bersk piece together what happened:

Jeremy was ambushed in the alleyway by an opponent he either hadn't seen coming or that hid its true power from him. It wasn't just faster and stronger than an elder vampyre–if that were the case, there should've been much, much more damage… The battle should've devastated several blocks.

But powerful demons could nullify the gifts of their descendants, including vampyres.

The elder demon ambushed Jeremy, nullified his power, then toyed with him. It kept the slaughter contained to an empty alleyway.

Jeremy knew he was going to die. In the end, all he could do was toss his Blood Promise across the slums and hope that another vampyre found it.

Bersk walked the alley to find the end of Jeremy's trail–it wasn't far.

The trail culminated in a single blight–the mix of blue tinged darkness and blood in the mud giving the appearance of a bruise upon the city. Jeremy had utterly vanished from the realm. With the sight of the Gray Queen, he would've seen the presence of any deadly magic that was responsible, but there was no trace of magic.

There was another explanation…

When demons crossed over, they were often weak and in need of sustenance. Most would start with small animals or children, as the brilgura in Keld had done, but powerful demons wouldn't be content with such a meal.

Jeremy had been eaten. *The poor bastard.*

Footsteps sounded from behind them, and Tam gasped.

Bersk turned to see Tam backing up toward him. Two men were stalking down the alley. Bersk had been so caught up in the scene that he—and Archimedes—had missed their approach.

But now Bersk saw them–saw *all* of them with the spell of his goddess. They were young men, not vampyres. Their clothes were lined with sweat and specks of dried ale. Each held a long knife in hand and a vicious smile on their face. Contrary to their demeanor, their blades were clean–unused.

"What's the matter, love?" the first said. "We just want some coin…"

A breath later, both men's gazes turned from the bard to the hunter whose eyes were dripping with blue magic. They stopped in their tracks, looking as if they'd seen a ghost.

Bersk stepped forward until he stood in front of Tam. The world grew dark as Bersk let his spell of sight fade.

Then he conjured *Twitch*. Fear and blue shone in the men's eyes.

"We didn't mean nothing by it, sir—"

"Yes, you did," Bersk replied.

They turned and ran, slipping in the muck of the alley.

Bersk let them go, let their whimpers fade away into the night. He willed *Twitch* away.

"There's been enough blood spilt."

Beside him, Tam chuckled. "Serves you right—" He quieted his voice. "Serves them right."

~

Bersk woke at morning to find Tam still sleeping and snoring quietly. He was surprised to see the bard had gotten any sleep at all, and resolved to go by himself to the Askcaster church. But as Bersk began putting on his leather armor, Tam startled from sleep.

"*What is it?* What's happening?

"Just going to church."

Tam propped himself up and looked around hastily. When he saw the sunlight streaming through the window, he collapsed back onto the bed. "Thank the gods for that. Wake me when you get back."

Bersk chuckled as he finished pulling leather covers over his forearms. "What happened to being afraid of being alone?"

"It's daylight. Bloody daylight. Noone's prowling around now."

Bersk left his partner to sleep and locked the door behind him, then strode out of the inn. The church of Arkcaster loomed across the river, so Bersk threaded traffic across the cobbles and the drawbridge. Archimedes cawed from the rooftops and followed.

Compared to the sweeping vista of the Septriones Church, the branch in Arkcaster was both small and utilitarian. It was scarcely larger than a block and only as high as the other buildings. Rather than intricate stonework and stained glass, the church was plain and with barred windows befitting an outpost or a stronghold. The modern Church was an important ally politically and militarily, so the structure wasn't surprising.

But the amount of people around *was*.

The church of Arckaster was swarming with Terrans. Town guards and soldiers surrounded the building, and Bersk saw several Knights of Kripishi intermingled with them. They worked together to control a flood of officials and gathering bystanders.

Bersk walked up next to the line of people and heard the mention of a *demon* half a dozen times before he made it to the front door. Bersk shook his head.

"So much for keeping things quiet," he muttered. At least he wouldn't have to waste time with subtlety.

A burly guard stepped forward to meet him. "State your name and business."

"Kevril Bersk, sent from Septriones Church by Pater O'Malley and Columen Devery. I bring word about the demon."

The guard rolled his eyes. "You and my mum, too."

Before Bersk could voice protest, a Knight stepped forward. "Bersk is okay to go in. Come with me."

The Knight pushed past the crowd without fanfare. Once inside, she pulled off her helmet, revealing dark, short-cropped hair.

There were more soldiers and Knights just inside the main doors. Even with a cursory glance, Bersk could *feel* the energy between them—they were on edge. And if Bersk had to guess, it wasn't about the crowd just outside.

"You look ready for war," Bersk said from behind.

"It's been… an interesting few days," she muttered.

Bersk followed her through the main hall to the congregation room in the back of the building.

The crowd had thinned significantly, but there were still two dozen priests, knights, and town officials. Instead of lofty sermons, voices rose and fell as church and townsmen tried to coordinate.

Some citystates were willing to work with the Church. From Bersk's perspective, most were wary of working with them. The Church's influence had only grown since Everdeath's crusade, and they were at the height of their power. Most cities were rightly worried about what control they might lose by conceding anything to the cloth.

Bersk understood those sacrifices better than most.

The knight led Bersk all the way up to the group, but waited respectfully for a lull in conversation to introduce him.

A frail priest with a long and equally wispy beard approached them. He spoke quickly to the knight and without looking at Bersk.

"Yes, yes. We've been expecting him. Pater O'Malley has sent me the details. In the meantime, he'll be working with myself and Noelle."

Finally, the priest turned to Bersk, "Have you any other updates since arriving?"

Carefully and without detail, Bersk told him of the missing vampyres.

"Eating them…" the priest muttered. "You better follow me."

~

The priest's name was Lurecine, and he led Bersk past the crowd and to a small study on the far side of the church.

"Don't mind the clutter," Lurecine said as he swung open the door.

Bersk froze and had to stifle a gasp. Not from the overpowering smell of parchment, but from the sight—

The priest's study was a glorified broom closet, containing little more than two chairs and a table between them. And it was absolutely littered with books and packed with loose paper. It was only because of Bersk's eyes as a hunter that he could see the furniture at all.

"Sit, sit," Lurecine said, ushering Bersk forward so that he could shut the door.

"Where?" Bersk muttered.

"Oh, just take those books and set them behind you."

Bersk sighed and picked up the three books from the guest chair. Rather than precariously balance them behind him, he sat with the books on his lap.

"O'Malley was right to send you to me," the priest said. "Come to Arkcaster and the first thing you do is work with vampyres…"

Bersk eyed the old priest, waiting for the inevitable backlash. That was the problem with the Church. They inevitably saw the world in black and white—the truth was shades of gray.

Pater Lurecine shuffled several stacks of paper and reorganized the books on his desk before settling on a single sheet.

"Look at that," he said, handing the paper to Bersk. It was a list of addresses for a mix of a dozen businesses and homes.

"Where did the vampyres disappear?" Lurecine asked.

"On the East side."

For the first time, Lurecine spoke slowly. "O'Malley tells me you're a tracker."

Bersk met his eyes. "I have my means." Somewhere on the roof of the church, a raven cawed.

The priest continued, "If we find a trail, can you follow it?"

Bersk nodded. Powerful demons warped the realm, like stretching out the fabric of a shirt. The longer they stayed in one spot, the larger the distortion. If Bersk could find the demon's last hideout, he could follow the trail from there.

If the demon was still in the city, then Bersk would find it.

Lurecine nodded. "Good. Arkcaster soldiers and the Order are scouting each of these locations. Once they're cleared, I need you to go to each of them. If there's a trail, alert us, *then* follow it."

There was a seriousness in the priest's voice as he spoke—one of parental advice and of necessity.

If the Church was using Bersk to find the demon's trail, it meant that their own tracking methods had failed them. Which only lended more weight to the theory that this elder demon was powerful—

That it was one of the Desolate Family.

Bersk suppressed a shiver. He would rather have been going up against Sircius Everdeath. For all the evil the lich wrought, he was only Terran.

~ ~ ~

Chapter 5
Checking Boxes

ONLY AN HOUR later, soldiers of Arkcaster and Knights of Kripishi were wading through the city streets. They fanned from the church and barracks outward in a coordinated raid.

Bersk followed behind, checking locations from the church outward and checking off locations on his copy of the addresses. Warehouses, graineries, shops—the first seven, empty. The only thing they found inside were frightened workers.

It wasn't until they crossed the river to the East side that they found anything at all.

A single butcher's barn out of a row, nestled between the outer wall of the city and the slums.

Bersk knew monsters, knew animals. They said that animals can sense when they were being led to slaughter or into a trap.

Some pigs struggled. Others quietly defecated themselves, as if they knew there was nothing they could do.

That was what Bersk felt of as he walked the alley, as he passed half a dozen soldiers and knights that couldn't hide the distress on their faces. It was deathly quiet—even the noise of the slums or occasional animal squeal died out as he approached the barn.

That's what they all felt.

A soldier stood out front and looked as if he wanted to say something, but he stammered over his words and stepped aside, defeated.

Bersk flexed the fingers of his right hand and the thought of his goddess quieted his mind—a little. He pushed open the door.

The barn was dominated by the single long butcher's block in the center and the many old blades hanging on the walls. A layer of sawdust was ground into the earth—no longer fresh.

And standing inside wrenched at his stomach like he was on the bow of the ship.

This was the place.

Again, Bersk called on the power of his goddess. *"Omni-videns ordinem,"* he said, and the power of *all-seeing order* tinged the world in blue—

And the barn in purple.

Old blood coated the floor. The ground was a deep purple marking the years where blood had seeped into the dirt. The tools were spackled with stains that no amount of water or soap could undo, and trails lined the walls where blood had dripped from the tools. The butcher's block had similar markings—purple stains seemed to carve deep in its face like rivers into a mountain.

But Bersk flinched as he tried to look upon the block itself. Even with the power of the Gray Queen running through him, his vision swam and again he felt a wave of nausea. At first, the spot merely looked hazy, but it felt as if the space in the center of the barn was a whirlpool. As if light itself was falling away.

His gaze passed over the void for only a moment, and in it he saw flashes of *Interregnum*—the realm between. The realm of the demons—

Walls of bones and suffering. Pools of liquid screams. Where the denizens breathed torture and worshipped pain.

It was forbidden to even read about Interregnum. Priests had committed suicide to rid themselves of the visions brought about by the unholy plane.

Even with the power of the Gray Queen, Bersk felt as if his mind had been placed upon the rack and the wheels were turning—stretching his mind until they would tear him apart.

Bersk turned and wretched onto the floor, then tried to still his breathing.

It wasn't the first time he'd seen the warped space and hints of Interregnum, but this was by far the deepest mark he'd seen; the only other that compared was in the home of a demon who'd lived there for *centuries*. One could tell the strength of the demon by the mark they left behind.

Bersk readied himself—he had a job to do.

He turned instead to the door and found the distortion stretching out into the alleyway, like a river of haze flowing through the air.

Bersk stepped into the alley. The other men and women flinched at the sight of his eyes, but he paid them no mind.

"Follow me," he ordered.

~

Kevril Bersk led a squad of Arkcaster soldiers and Knights of Kripishi through the alleys. Citizens backed against the walls to let them pass or scurried back into their homes. Bersk was vaguely aware that the guards were ordering people off the streets, but he kept his eyes and mind on the task.

The warped trail led them to the outer wall of the city. The bricks towered above them, blotting out the morning sun.

Bersk followed the trail all the way to an underground entrance. The old wooden doors were shut, but the lock was broken—tossed aside.

Archimedes called a warning from the top of the wall.

Bersk looked to the captain of the guard behind him. "Where does this lead?"

"To the catacombs. Then run beneath the whole city."

"This is where the trail leads. We need to scout the premise. I need ten of your best to go with me—soldiers *and* knights. Preferably ones who know the layout."

The captain nodded. "That'd be me." Then the grizzled soldier called out for more men while the knight in charge did the same. Then he called for runners to send word to the barracks and the church.

In moments, Bersk had his team. To their credit, they all put on a stoic face.

They would need it.

Bersk heaved open the doors. Behind him, the knights conjured floating lights. The orbs hovered just over their shoulders.

"Keep those at my back," the hunter ordered. He needed to be able to see the trail clearly, and their magic might affect it.

Bersk descended the stairs and stooped down beneath the low ceiling. At one point, the whole of the passageway might've been lined with brick, but now chunks had fallen away, revealing mortar and hard packed earth beneath; the air was stifling and pungent with the smell of it.

The passageway seemed to follow the outer wall of the city, then branched off toward the center of Arkcaster. That was where the trail of the elder demon led—toward the center of the city.

They passed two junctions before Bersk heard the whisper of familiar spells.

"Lux patris, consumat ferrum," muttered the knights. One by one, the light in the tunnels increased as their blades were consumed by glowing light.

The spell would be a boon against demons, but Bersk sighed at the waste. Right now, the spell would only drain the knights' stamina.

They had passed into the inner circles of the catacombs. Now, alcoves lined the walls where stacks of the dead had been laid to rest—some in ornate coffins, others merely wrapped and coated in resin. Carvings of names and histories lined the walls around them, but Bersk dared not look away from his task.

The trail was waning. The haze that marked the demon's passage had thinned to from a river to a trickle—little more than a wisp. But there were other signs…

Fresh blood glowed purple in Bersk's magic sight. It was smeared on the walls and sticky beneath the hunter's boots. Something had drawn on the walls with blood, designs that were too simple to be runes. They were abstract, like a child's drawing.

Berks's heart sank. His mind flashed to lesser demons—hunched and twisted—joyfully painting with the blood of their victims. The elder demon had already found the means to summon minions. It likely wasn't a fully formed rift—such a thing would warp space throughout the city above—but even a handful of lesser demons could overwhelm them.

They had to retreat. Now.

Then Bersk heard the first signs of life—footsteps. Bersk quickly held up a hand, signaling the men behind him to hold their positions.

As their shuffling stopped, so too did the footsteps somewhere in the catacombs.

The squad waited in eerie silence. So did their enemies.

Bersk motioned for the soldiers to move backward. Slowly and quietly, the squad moved back the way they'd come.

Though the magic lights wouldn't reach far, Bersk could see through the darkness to the bend in the hall. Eyes peeked out from around the corners and crept into the open.

Each lesser demon was vaguely Terran in shape, hunched over and walking on fours like monkeys, but every bit of them was *wrong*. They were covered in patches of matted fur. The rest of their skin glistened with blood and sweat. Too long limbs twisted at odd angles. Faces twisted into wide-eyed grins, mouths half full of teeth that cut their lips like daggers.

Bersk didn't waste a moment longer. He kept the *all-seeing order* spell and conjured speed. *"Astar na gaoithe.* Fall back, now! They're coming."

As the soldiers turned to run, the demons scurried down the hall after them.

With a thought, *Twitch* flashed into his hand.

More scurrying steps echoed through the tunnels. Shouts from the soldiers behind him.

The first of the demons lunged for Bersk, thin fingers grasped at his face. Bersk cut three times through it, *Twitch* little more than a blur as the demon fell to pieces.

But for as depraved and single-minded as lesser demons were, they had their own magic.

Infernal words came out, sounding somewhere between a dog's growl and a choking gasp. Tusks of bone sprouted from the walls and floor, twisting like snakes toward the men as they ran.

The Knights of Kripishi called out wards and counterspells, and again, Bersk's heart sank. The demons' spells should've crumbled to dust with the first uttering of holy power. Now they merely paused.

The elder demon's power had grown, and its influence was bolstering the lesser demons' power.

Worse, their retreat had slowed—they'd been surrounded—and now men at the front had to fight their way through.

As they retreated, Bersk could spare only a moment to look at the other men. The Knights of Kripishi had spread out amongst the group, each using magic to protect themselves and the Arkcaster soldiers between them. Even in that short moment, Bersk saw the fighters' resolve winning out over panic.

Then came a sound like the patter of rain.

"Amalgamation!" a knight at the front screamed.

Bersk turned and pushed his way through the group of men, urging them to cover the rear in his absence.

They were nearly at the last junction and if they could make it past, then they would survive. But the amalgamation was coming from the right, threatening to smash through them and cut off retreat for the back half of the group.

The knights would have magic to fend off smaller foes, but they could do nothing against more powerful demons—not without priests and saints.

Bersk pushed through, shouting and grasping for the tower shield of the nearest soldier—wrenching the man's arm in the process. He slipped the shield over his left arm and muttered the words for strength.

"Vires et voluntatem." Power flowed into his muscles. Where once his blade had been swift, now he stood with the strength of ten men. Bersk stepped into the side hall and raised his shield defiantly.

Then he uttered, *"Mora ordinem,"* and *Twitch* dripped with violent blue power.

Bersk could no longer see through the darkness as if it was daylight, but he could see far enough with the knights' light at his back.

And he saw horror.

A wall of flesh crawled toward him—its long centipedal body made from dozens of demons merged together. It crawled toward him using whole bodies of single demons as legs, crushing faces and ribs with each step—shattering coffins as it clawed at the walls. The fevered screams of the individuals held it together in a mass of suffering.

Bersk channeled all his strength and magic into holding his shield and holding his ground.

The amalgamation slammed into his shield, and even with bolstered strength he was pushed back across the bricks. Bersk groaned—yelled. Hands and feet and faces reached around the shield for him.

As soon as the beast slowed, Bersk swung Twitch around the shield, slashing wildly at anything he could reach. Each slash left a scalding wound in the creature as the power of his goddess burned it away. If it was possible, the amalgamation's screams grew louder, and soon blue power mixed with demonic blood and dripped to the floor around him.

It wasn't enough. Bersk fought for footing, but inch by inch, he slid back. Brick cracked, and the shield groaned.

There might've been a foot between him and the end of the hall where the other men fought for their lives.

"We're through!" came a shout of salvation.

Bersk kept his feet planted until he felt a tap on the shoulder from another knight. "Come on, Bersk!"

He didn't need any other encouragement.

Bersk let the weight of the amalgamation shove him back into the hall and he sprinted after the rest of the squad.

Behind him, the crunch of bones sounded as other demons were trampled beneath the monster's bulk and as it plodded after them. But the amalgamation was slow, and they easily outran it.

Bersk bounded up the short stairs and out of the catacombs, leaving the screams behind.

Bersk willed away *Twitch* and shut the doors. Someone had fetched a length of chain and looped it through the handles, then locked it.

"Will that hold them?" one of the Arkcaster soldiers asked.

No one had escaped unscathed. Several men shoved fists under the plates of their armor to slow bleeding. Others were covered in demon blood—Bersk was one of the latter.

Bersk nodded and tried to reassure them. "They won't come into the light."

Thumps sounded against the doors, shaking and splintering the wood. Bersk could see flesh moving behind the new cracks, and moments later, the demons receded.

Bersk added, "They won't come into the light for now."

Another knight said, "Not while their master is below. But this will keep any unfortunate souls from wandering down there."

The captain of the soldiers shook his head. "We need to get word to our superiors. We're going to need more men."

Bersk said, "We'll need priests and a saint if we have one."

One of the other soldiers muttered, "A godsdamn company of soldiers."

~ ~ ~

Chapter 6
Pieces

SANTA ANNA WAS led to the Septriones judiciary room in magic shackles and dressed in a plain white robe. She wouldn't be allowed to wear her vestments until the trial had concluded. Archleon Greghan and the other presiding officials thought it would give her too much sway over the jury of her peers.

The saint walked with her head held high, despite the accusations heaped upon her. She had faith that her peers would see to reason, just as she had seen.

Some years ago, Anna had presided over a similar trial, though one purely criminal and not blasphemous in nature. A young priest had embezzled money from his conclave.

It did pain her to be treated in the same fashion as a common criminal such as that, but Anna would never admit it. Not even to fellow saints. Not even to Kevril Bersk.

And she would never show it. Never let anyone see her facade crack.

The judiciary wing of the Septriones church was on the second floor of the main building, and so she was escorted through a sea of onlookers from the main floor all the way up the stairs—priests and diocese from neighboring towns and cities that had the means to travel.

Worse to Anna were the gold drapings of Septriones. She had almost forgotten how gaudy the Church dressed itself. Her time in the ruins of Mecendu and imprisoned below ground had changed her perspective, that least of all.

Guards pushed open the imposing double doors to the judiciary room and ushered her inside. Stained glass windows depicting scenes from the Enchiridion took up much of the walls, as if hoping to remind the accused of their *lost morals*.

Archleons and columen filled the room. They represented an extraordinary number of Church leadership. Even Santa Glory and Saint Ozemon were in attendance. Though the pair met her eyes, they gave no reassuring smile or condescending frowns—such things were above them.

Most of the other Church leadership were equally composed, save perhaps Archleon Greghan and Columen Devery who were opposing emotions in the crowd.

Archleon Haldack stepped up to the judge's chair. He was a stonecutter before the cloth, a squat man with a powerful build that showed even beneath his vestments. Weathered by neither age nor service. Santa Anna had never met him, but his demeanor matched him, and he emanated control as he motioned for everyone to take their seats and places.

Santa Anna took her place on the left side of the room, next to Columen Devery. Though the trial and judiciary room itself only moderately resembled a governmental trial, for all purposes, her side was that of *the Accused*. Those that sat behind her would be composed of clergy willing to hear her side and those that believed in her position of sainthood.

Those on the other side of the room believed in the immutability of scripture and the rule of law. They would be against her.

Archleon Haldack cleared his throat and addressed the room.

"We are gathered today to determine the fate of one, Santa Anna. To determine whether her decision to visit the Frozen Isles and the ruins of Mecendu were righteous or in error.

"Sainthood is the highest mark of the cloth and though they are conduits of the light, their decisions must be weighed against the good of the realm and the good of the Church.

"Her records from sainthood until the day of her expedition are barred from the record and shall have no bearing on these proceedings.

"Some months ago, Santa Anna used her station to commandeer the ship, the *Barrel Eye*, departed the Arkcaster, and sailed for the Frozen Isles. There she knowingly entered into the territory of Traasmouth. Traasmouth is a sovereign nation who has rebuked the light of the Church and barred entry to citizens of Arkcaster, Hunson, and Torreleigh, of which Santa Anna hails from.

"Furthermore, when Santa Anna sought permission from her peers for her journey, she was explicitly denied permission and went against the wishes of the Church.

"Lastly, Santa Anna traveled to the ruins of Mecendu inside the borders of Traasmouth. These ruins are sacred sites, both to the Church and to Traasmouth. The tenuous history of the ruins is a prominent factor in Traasmouth's rebuke of our light."

As Archleon Haldack finished, a harsh silence fell over the room. He breathed deeply, as if drawing in strength.

"Santa Anna, these are grave charges, any one of which could wear heavily on your sainthood or strip you of the position. How do you plead?"

Anna stood as Leo Haldack addressed her. She felt the eyes of a hundred believers fall upon her, and many more through the scrying constructs throughout the room. Thousands might have been watching—

Many of whom had already decided her guilt.

She stood tall, for she was certain that the evidence she found would absolve her.

Santa Anna said, loud enough for all to hear, "I plead righteousness."

Haldack turned to the prosecution on the other side of the room. "And how do you plead?"

Archleon Greghan rose. He, too, spoke loud enough for all to hear. "We propose that the accused acted in grievous error of her station."

Haldack asked, "Please list the evidence."

"We have eyewitness testimony of her *forcible* departure from port of Arkcaster and her commandeering of the *Barrel Eye*. Traasmouth reached out to the nearest Church about her violation of their territory and her plundering of the ruins of Mecendu. And, *of course*, Santa Anna was apprehended in the sacred site itself."

Anna resisted the urge to glare at Leo Greghan as he finished. Silently, she reminded herself that the Archleon couldn't help the smugness from creeping into his voice—

And she prayed for the same resolve that presiding Leo Haldack possessed.

Haldack turned to Anna. "Santa Anna, do you dispute any of the charges or evidence levied against you?"

"I'm just waiting for you to ask what I found." Her palms felt clammy as the words left her lips. It was a comment unbecoming of her, but it had slipped out.

A smirk crossed Haldack's face and was just as quickly stricken from record. "Don't worry. We'll get to that."

~ ~

VARNEY BARRIS SPENT the last two nights talking to every vampyre he knew.

Well, almost every vampyre. There would be plenty that wouldn't see things reasonably. He didn't bother with Elder Aspet or Elder Lorith or their cabals.

But Varney was willing to bet that *most* vampyres would see things reasonably. Especially after they had seen what he had seen.

The vampyre pulled his hood forward, shielding his eyes from the morning sun. He was old enough now that he could go out without fear of being scalded alive, but he still didn't bloody well *like it*. One day he'd walk the daylight like a true elder—sun on his face and pride in his heart.

Varney paused as he rounded the alley corner. If what the demon said was true, then there'd be no more daylight. Every demon-blooded would walk the realm free as damn birds.

"Doesn't seem fair," Varney muttered to himself as he continued toward the catacomb entrance. He'd had to wait *three bloody lifetimes* to just to fart in the sun.

He skulked through the alleys, shoving past low lives that didn't have the sense to get out of his way and showing his fangs to those stupid enough to mouth off about it.

There were no less than fifteen entrances to the catacombs beneath the city, and Varney made a point never to use the same one in a row. He stopped at the one on the South side of the city, pulled a key out of his pocket, and let himself in.

He crept onto the stairs and shut the doors behind him, then descended into the dark. The air on this side of the passages was muggier for some reason, which always struck him as at, since there were other entrances closer to the river—

But Varney only spared it a passing thought.

Because as soon as the doors shut behind him, he heard the pitter patter of demonic feet. Varney stood still in the dim light and let the ankle biters come to him. They ambled toward him, half-spider, half-monkey, their mangled faces in perpetual sneers.

Whereas their master unnerved Varney on a primal level, he felt only revulsion for these pitiful creatures. They were little more than animals—even a vampyre in the midst of starvation had more resolve and composure than these *things*.

They scurried around Varney, sniffing and chattering at him while they clambered over one another. Varney started walking after a few moments—after Varney *knew* they recognized him—but they still swarmed around him like a school of twisted fish.

The strangest thing was that Varney could smell a little of the master's sweet scent on them. It was just a hint, and he doubted that any lesser vampyres would recognize it under the smell of filth and blood, but it was curious and absurd thing—

Was the demonic realm a sweet-smelling place? did the demons marinate in it as they grew older and more powerful? Or was the scent a byproduct of their power?

Varney smirked at the thoughts and walked faster, both eager to get the audience with the elder demon over and excited to smell him again. His steps quickened the nearer he got to the center of the crypt tunnels, passing rows and rows of dead too short-sighted to seek immortality.

This time, he noticed that more of the tunnels were blurring together with the demonic realm. The walls had turned into a spackle of bones and a wallpaper of skin. By the time Varney reached the center, his boots squelched on the mixture of muscle and flesh that covered the stone floor. It even pulsed beneath his feet like a cow shaking off flies.

Weirdly enough, these early tunnels didn't smell in the slightest: Not rotten, not bloody, not sweet. That last fact depressed Varney somewhat, but he always had the elder demon to look forward to.

Decades ago, vampyres used to congregate down in the crypts—not just for rituals and initiations. The first blood dens were set up down here. As Varney entered the central chamber of the crypts, it was hard to imagine the way it had been.

It used to be a spacious chamber; the walls lined with the skeletons and urns of noble families. A dozen altars were spread across the floor, always decorated with flowers and trinkets giving recognition to the dead.

Now it looked like a grotesque garden. There were rows of things that looked like a mix of flowers and hands growing from the flesh of the floor. The walls were lined with vines of intestines and mantles of ribs and pelvises. Skulls littered the floor like decorative stones.

And at the center of it all, the elder demon knelt before an enormous altar of bone. His arms and neck were bent at unnatural angles as he gave thanks to the mother of all demons, Ariazi—also, the grandmother of all vampyres.

It wasn't until Varney stepped past the threshold that marked the center of the crypt that he smelled the overpowering scent of sulfur and the elder demon's sickly sweet aroma.

Varney waited respectfully at the edge of the room for the demon to finish. He'd been called many insults over his long life, but one thing he'd never been called was disrespectful. He steadied his breathing and tried not to pay attention to how hard his twisted heart was pounding.

He spared a single glance back to see where the lesser demons had gone. They were sitting patiently at the threshold of the room—staring at him with wide, unblinking eyes. They had never crossed into the center chamber.

When the elder demon finished, his arms and neck twisted back into position with violent pops and snaps.

Still facing the altar, the demon said, "Come here, Varney Barris."

The vampyre walked quickly over to the elder's side. Living in the city had done the creature well, Varney decided. His shoulders had thickened and his face had filled out from his frequent meals. Even his hair had filled in a bit.

"Did you bring what I asked?"

"Yes, sir," Varney said, patting his vest pocket. Holy water corrupted by the blood of Interregnum.

"Good. Now give thanks."

Varney's eyes climbed up the bone altar and he suddenly felt small and pitiful—a childlike fear welled up in him, and the words came out a croak. "Oh, Ariazi, mother of my mother, flesh of my flesh—"

"Not with words, Varney," the demon whispered.

Varney's eyes widened, but when he tried to turn his head to question the elder, Varney realized that he couldn't move—

Then his body moved of its own accord.

His arms rose, snaking upward until they were nearly stretched out overhead. His elbows twisted around, wrenching his shoulders out of their sockets. Varney grimaced as his knees did similarly.

Varney grit his teeth, desperate not to cry out—convinced that crying out would bring the elder's wrath upon him—but he couldn't suppress a whimper. The vampyre fell to his knees. His head shook violently and his neck gave way with a pop. Mercifully, he could no longer feel the anguish of supplication.

His body shuddered violently for another minute, and then it began to untwist itself. His arms reset, his legs turned around the correct way.

His neck was last. It settled back into place with three quick pops—

Then the feeling came back to his body, and Varney collapsed in a whimpering pile.

~ ~

KEVRIL BERSK WAITED somewhat patiently outside the Arkcaster barracks. The captain was inside, pleading the case to leadership to mobilize everything they had alongside the Church and the Knights of Kripishi in order to assault the catacombs beneath the city.

The sun was now high in the sky and he'd been outside at least for an hour waiting. Bersk knew enough about bureaucracy to know that waiting this long wasn't a good sign.

So he'd sent Archimedes to fetch Tam and bring him across the city.

Bersk watched Archimedes swoop low over the crowd and perch on the top of the barracks. Shortly after, Tamren Jorbough threaded through the crowd toward Bersk.

"You know, it's bloody difficult to follow Archimedes through Arkcaster," Tam said, fixing his shirt and neckerchief. "The buildings are too high," he added, miming for emphasis.

Bersk allowed himself a short-lived chuckle. He had reservations about what he was about to ask of Tam, but he couldn't chance missing the call to mobilize.

"Uh oh," Tam muttered. "You have that look about you."

Bersk replied, "I just need you to run an errand or two while I'm waiting." Bersk gestured toward the barracks.

Tam scoffed. "Waiting for what? For the demons to send a written invitation to their lair?"

"Something like that. They're holed up beneath the city, and *as always*, the wheels of bureaucracy are slow to turn."

"I'll run any number of errands for you, so long as I don't have to go under there and see *him* again."

"You should choose your words more carefully," Bersk muttered.

"Why? …What do you need me to do?"

Bersk pulled the Blood Promise necklace from his vest pocket and handed it to Tam. "I need you to find Lorith, and tell her that her brother's dead."

Tam's face paled and he stared off across Arkcaster for a long moment before taking the necklace. "I *should* choose my words more carefully. Perhaps she didn't like the man, and she'll be happy to hear that he's bit his last bite?"

"I don't think so," Bersk replied, "but I'm hoping she and the other elders will be sympathetic to our plight. I need you to convince her to join us… We're going to need all the help we can get."

"An enemy of my enemy… I suppose. I hope she's hungry for revenge and not thirsty for, well, me."

"Are you alright, Tam?"

The bard scoffed and tried to fake bravado. "Of course! I love delivering good news to creatures that might otherwise eat me."

"It's just that you make bad jokes when you're nervous."

Tam swallowed. "You see right through me, Bersk. …Do you think the old *Sanctuary* spell will work on her?"

Bersk nodded. "I think so. Besides, I think she's smart enough not to make enemies of us while there's bigger problems. The demon killed her brother, after all."

~ ~ ~

Chapter 7
Gameboard

TAMREN JORBOUGH SKIRTED the city streets back toward the *Les Enfants Terribles* blood den. This time Archimedes followed him.

The psychopomp wouldn't be able to go with Tam into the blood den itself, but Bersk assured him that it would wait outside—hopefully not to avenge him.

Tam really wasn't too frightened of his current situation or of Lorith. She had seemed reasonable enough. But no matter how much he knew that intellectually, he couldn't still his racing heart or his clammy hands. He was still walking into a proverbial lion's den—without Bersk.

He rounded the corner of the street, passing the tailor and cobbler's shops. No one was outside hawking their wares today. In fact, it seemed as if the entire city was on edge—

everyone spoke in hushed tones and walked quickly through the streets.

Tam reminded himself to get a new vest when all this was done, and to give that young lad a cut of it. If he made it out of all this.

He went around to the charred door and turned the knob—committing himself to task as the metal heated in his hand. Finally, it turned all the way around and Tam pushed through to the staircase cloaked in darkness.

Tam cleared his throat, and said, *"Primum sanctuarium."* A warmness enveloped him, one that succeeded—at least a little—in pushing back the sense of oppression and foreboding.

As long as Tam did nothing to provoke or anger the vampyres, they shouldn't be able to attack him—that was how the old shaman had explained it years ago.

Still, the spell was a small comfort as the bard descended the staircase to *Les Enfants Terribles.*

A hand grabbed his shoulder.

Tam froze and looked out of the corner of his eye to see a figure stepping out of the darkness that lined the stairs.

~ ~

IMPATIENCE GOT THE better of Kevril Bersk. The hunter jostled his way into the Arkcaster church under the guise of speaking with Pater Lurecine.

Bersk was half-surprised when it worked. At least the Church was taking the issue of demons beneath the city serious enough not to worry about a former Knight forcing his way inside.

The church was packed with Arkcaster soldiers, town guards, priests, knights, and other officials, and the crowd only got thicker as Bersk moved toward the congregation room in the back of the building. Despite the crowd, only a few were speaking, and Bersk could hear them clearly.

"We're waiting for word from Gerhull. We need more priests and columen!" an old archleon said.

A priest responded, "Leo, there is no time."

"We need to consider other options!" a soldier said, voice raising—the captain from the catacombs

Another archleon replied, "Not those options. Absolutely not."

Bersk slowly worked his way forward, and after a moment, found Pater Lurecine in the crowd. The old priest met his eyes, then walked around the edge of the room toward him.

Bersk leaned close to the priest. "What *really* is there to discuss?"

Lurecine sighed and led them out of the crowd and to his study. Bersk set aside a stack of papers and sat, feeling even more claustrophobic inside the old man's office.

"They're trying to decide what to do," Lurecine said wearily.

"I see that, but we don't have time for this. There are demons beneath the city."

"They know. The attending diocese want to wait for reinforcements from Gerhull. Columen Jonn won't admit it in front of the others, but he's afraid. This is unprecedented, Bersk."

Bersk rolled his eyes. "I thought columen were supposed to embody the boldness of the Light?"

Lurecine chuckled gravely. "Yes, well…"

"What other plans do they have besides waiting?"

"The commander wants to use the river to flood the catacombs. The Church will have nothing of it, of course. There's too much history that would be lost."

"What about the risk to the city?"

"A little water never hurt anything. Apparently, the commander went to the smiths before bringing the idea to the diocese. They say that once the demons are gone, they can just pump the catacombs dry again… Why are you looking like that?"

Bersk met the priest's eyes. He must've been smiling. "Because flooding the catacombs just might work. It won't kill the elder demon, but it will disrupt whatever ritual it's planning and it might destroy the lesser demons without dirtying our hands."

Lurecine shook his head. "They won't do it, Bersk. They won't sacrifice hundreds of years of history."

"If that thing beneath us really is one of the Desolate Family, then we can't pull any punches. More than just Arkcaster or some long dead priests are on the line. What's the point in preserving the past if we have no future?"

Bersk stood and shuffled past the stacks of books and paper, the gobsmacked priest, and into the packed congregation room. He shuffled to the back of the group, where the upper ranks of soldiers, guards, and diocese were still arguing.

The hunter grit his teeth and cleared his throat. Then he spoke over the archleon, "Who's in charge here?"

All eyes nearby swiveled toward him, most of them dismissively.

"I am," a tall archleon said. "And who—"

"*I am,*" a stout soldier interrupted. "Commander Zin. And who are you, knight?"

The archleon scoffed, "He's no knight of ours."

Another man pushed forward to the front. He wore the orange sash to denote him as a captain and had a long scar down the right side of his face that cut through his hairline and the line of his beard.

Bersk recognized Captain Henring—the commanding officer who'd stumbled upon the hive of the Formicae.

Henring pointed at Bersk, "This is Kevril Bersk, the hunter who fought alongside our brigade. He was there when the demon stepped foot onto our plane, and he destroyed the altar!"

The archleon sneered, "Alongside the vampyres, Captain?"

Commander Zin shot a scowl in the direction of the archleon. "That's enough, Leo Victus." Then he nodded to Bersk. "What do you have to say?"

"You cannot wait, sir. Lesser demons infest the catacombs and are already merging into amalgamations. Soon, the demonic realm will bleed through the walls of the catacombs. Once that, happens you won't just be rooting demons out of the cellar… you'll be fighting off an invasion."

Leo Victus said, "If the situation is as dire as you say, then we need reinforcements. No amount of soldiers or knights will be enough."

Bersk met the archleon's gaze. "Muster your diocese then. Serve the people as you claim to."

Victus's face twisted into a scowl. A few of the surrounding diocese shared his notion, but most looked shocked at the statement.

"Leave this church."

Bersk didn't flinch, but before he could answer, Commander Zin said to Bersk, "You're dismissed, Kevril Bersk, but don't go far. We're marching on the East wing *immediately*, and we'll need your help."

Commander Zin turned back to the diocese. "We're flooding the catacombs, with or without you. The demons won't get another nightfall beneath Arkcaster."

Bersk turned as the congregation room devolved into cheers and shouts, evenly divided along party lines. He tried not to let the satisfaction show on his face.

~ ~

SANTA ANNA HALF-LISTENED while the presiding Archleon Haldack led the judiciary room in a short prayer. It was customary for all trials, but she'd half expected Leo Greghan to object to it as well.

Her prosecutor sat forward in his seat, even in prayer, as if ready to object to anything.

Haldack's prayer asked for the Light to illuminate the truth.

That's exactly what she would do next.

"Light be upon us," Haldack finished. "Now, Santa Anna will offer her testimony as to the righteousness of her actions, that her reasons overshadowed the will of her peers and the will of Traasmouth's sovereignty. What say you?"

Anna rose and again felt a hundred sets of eyes and scrying constructs focusing on her.

"Before I left Eadruin, I had a vision. In it, I saw the end of our world—"

Leo Greghan stood. "Objection. The counsel already knows of this *supposed* vision, but it's hardly worthy of testimony. Numerous saints have visions—"

"Overruled," Haldack said from the podium. "Santa Anna will be permitted to state her vision to the many *that have not heard it.*"

Anna stilled herself and continued, "In my vision, I walked streets of Penelope, Sangrimore, Nontir, and the capital. The cobbles were made of bone, and rivers were filled with blood and bile. Our home twisted into a grotesque mirror of Interregnum—the realm between. The air was thick with screams and suffering was the only language we knew." Merely speaking of the vision brought a chill that she couldn't suppress. "I assure you that no amount of scripture or testimony can prepare you for such a vision.

"Act six details three apocalypses, including the the World of Blood," Anna said. "They tell us the events that will precede the rise of the demons, but they do not divulge when the events will start or how the demons will take over. That is what I sought to find out."

Leo Haldack cleared his throat. "This inquiry is what you brought to the diocese?"

"Yes, and I was denied."

"You went to the ruins to seek those answers? But we have holy sites in Eadruin that might've held the answers…"

Anna replied, "Those sites are held under strict control by the Church." Because they contain writings that contradict the Enchiridion.

Greghan spoke up, "She means that they would not allow her access because the diocese had already denied her those options."

Anna said, "The diocese had made their decision clear. They had denied the importance of my premonition and denied my access to any holy sites on *every continent.*"

Greghan raised his voice, "She was denied because her vision couldn't be corroborated by any other saints, and because those holy sites are strictly forbidden to everyone, including saints."

Archleon Haldack raised a hand to silence the prosecution. "Santa Anna, why did you seek out those ruins specifically?"

Anna replied, "There were other locations on the mainlands, but the ruins of Mecendu were the most remote. There would be the least chance that my peers or even Mecendu would interfere with my research."

Greghan spoke out again, "Do you see the lengths she went too—"

Anna spoke louder, "The lengths I went to for righteousness! For the survival of our world."

Haldack slammed his gavel down. "That's enough Santa Anna. Leo Greghan, I can see your passion for the Church, but practice your humility when it's not your turn to speak."

~ ~

"I'VE BEEN WAITING for you, Tamren Jorbough."

Tam winced at his name and the cold hand gripping his shoulder. But as his heart raced, the grip relaxed—

Lorith stepped out from the darkness and stood beside him on the stairs. Tam let out a breath he didn't realize he'd been holding, but Lorith's expression was hard and urgent.

"Come," she said. "It's not safe for you here. We can talk in your room at the inn."

Tam let out the rest of his breath and chuckled awkwardly. A woman taking him back to his room wasn't how he envisioned today going. Then again, it was a better development than a vampyre taking him back to their place...

"What's wrong?" the vampyre asked.

Tam quickly shook his head. "Nothing. You just gave me a fright. Come on."

Tam turned around and led Lorith back up the dark stairs and out into the alley.

And immediately froze.

Four men and women surrounded him—two standing directly in front of the door, and one to either side. It wasn't so much the smell of blood or filth emanating from them that told Tam they were vampyres, nor the fangs they didn't bother to hide.

It was their eyes. One by one, as Tam looked at them, they stared back with a wide-eyed intensity that he had only seen in monsters.

Lorith stepped up the final stairs and stood quietly beside him.

All four vampyres took a step back.

The man in front with greasy, swept-back hair bowed to her. "Elder Lorith, we—we didn't expect you." When he stood upright, he didn't meet her eyes.

She looked at each of them in turn, and Tam thought he saw a hint of a scowl cross her lips.

"Chanteclaire," Lorith said. "I see you're still doing Varney's dirty work."

"Shouldn't all children serve their masters?"

"So long as it doesn't get them killed… This one is with me," she said, gesturing to Tam. "You may tell Varney that I did him the favor of letting his children live."

"Elder Lorith… I'm sorry." The young vampyre began trembling. "I'm not here under Varney Barris's command."

There was a sudden rush of air and a violent snap. It happened so fast that Tam couldn't be sure what happened—only that when he opened his eyes, one of the young vampyres lay at Tam's feet. Dead.

It had attacked and moved so fast that Tam couldn't see it. Tam's fear redoubled.

Lorith rolled her shoulders and clasped her hands in front of her, patiently waiting.

"Then who ordered you to your death?" she asked.

Again, there was a maelstrom of action. Tam squeezed his eyes shut. It was all over in a breath.

Two other vampyres had attacked and been cut down. They lay bleeding and unmoving on the dirt. Lorith had the last vampyre—Chanteclaire—by the throat and on his knees, throat bulging in her grasp. He feebly clawed at Lorith's wrist.

Lorith's eyes grew pale. "I *command* you, young one. Tell me who controls you."

Tam watched as the paleness left her eyes and then overtook the young vampyre. Where hers had been only cloudy, Chanteclaire's eyes turned white as milk—the color completely gone.

Lorith relaxed her grip, just enough for him to speak. Chanteclair's face twisted up to meet her eyes.

"The maw—the maw of his mother. The—the right hand of Ari—"

Chanteclair had struggled to speak until his head twisted around so violently that his body was thrown across the alley.

Tam lurched backward and looked to Lorith, but she looked as startled as he was. She stood, hand still outstretched—now empty.

After a moment, she relaxed. "There are penalties when a vampyre goes against their master's wishes. Chanteclaire wasn't supposed to speak of him…"

Tam's revulsion settled enough for him to understand. The poor bastard had been caught between two commands, and he had paid for it.

"I've never seen a compulsion strong enough to kill," Lorith added. "Come. We can't stay here."

Tam nodded quickly.

"You've got red on you," she said, offering him a handkerchief. "Clean yourself up before we go out onto the streets. I hope you'll have better news when we reach your room."

Tam swallowed the lump in his throat and dabbed his face. The handkerchief came back with streaks of blood.

~ ~ ~

Chapter 8
Choose Carefully

AFTER THE AMBUSH, Tam and Lorith walked the cobbles of Arkcaster back to the inn.

Just since the morning, the crowds were growing noticeably thinner. Tam passed shuttered storefront after storefront, which had given rise to which: Did the stores close first, or did they see how few shoppers were around and close after?

The truth was much simpler—word was getting around that things were not alright in Arkcaster. Tam could see it in the way people shuffled about, glancing warily toward the alleys and over their shoulders. Paranoia had seized the city.

Neither the bard nor the elder vampyre spoke until they got back to inn and shut the door behind them.

"Now then. I suspect you'll want to know about your brother," Tam said, throat tightening. When Lorith nodded, he pulled the Blood Promise necklace from his pocket and forced himself to continue. "We found the last trace of your brother. It was the demon."

Lorith took the necklace and gazed upon it fondly. "Stop. Did he… Was it quick?"

"Yes," Tam lied. Lorith didn't look at him, and for that, he was grateful. "…Are you alright?"

"Are you asking me that because I'm a woman, Mr. Jorbough? I'm old enough to be your grandmother's grandmother."

Tam smiled softly. "You've aged quite well, but no. I ask because you lost your brother and grief shows clearly no matter our years."

Lorith clutched the necklace and nodded. "I'm not so cold that I don't grieve, but I'd said goodbye to my brother a thousand times in a thousand ways. The thread that bound us together was already frayed and a small thing to sever.

"The demon will pay," she said decisively. She draped her brother's necklace around her neck and tucked it in her blouse. Tam saw the edge of a second, similar chain—presumably Lorith's own necklace.

She wiped her eyes with a handkerchief and asked, "How can I help?"

Tam smirked. "I'm afraid Bersk is the one for that question. He was requesting the help of the Arkcaster military and the Church of First Light."

"And they're dragging their feet," she finished.

"Which is why Bersk sent me to you."

Lorith stood and stared off at the wall in thought. "I'll beseech the other elders…" She turned to Tam. "Your sanctuary spell was a nice touch, but it won't save you."

"What do you mean?"

"It will save you from the lesser turned, but it won't save you if an elder is commanded to attack you."

Tam suddenly felt cold and clammy. He stared at Lorith, waiting for her to elaborate.

Lorith added, "A great many of the elders are loyal to the dark scriptures, and the lesser turned will be unable to resist the demon—they'll bow like a field of grass in the wind. Only the elders stand a chance of fighting subjugation... but I suspect most of the elders are already siding with the demon. They'll think that by voluntarily serving it that they'll be spared, that they'll keep their faculties and free will... They're wrong. If he is really the son of Ariazi, they will be no sparing any of us."

~ ~

VARNEY BARRIS WATCHED from the alleys as Arkcaster guards and priests of the Church of First Light gathered on the streets.

In all his years, he'd never seen them coordinate.

After all, they were two opposing factions of Arkcaster. The soldiers, the guards, and the politicians, who represented the citizens, or so they told themselves. And then there was the Church of First Light, who represented the Church and whatever else.

The vampyre watched, a drip of saliva falling from his lips. He didn't bother to wipe it away. He wasn't sure what the two factions were planning, but he was damn sure that it wouldn't matter.

Even if the soldiers and priests *could* fight their way through the catacombs and stop the demon, they weren't going to have time.

The third powerful faction of Arkcaster was gathering in the shadows and alleys, readying an ambush. Dozens of vampyres had joined the demon's cause—some by choice. Most had been enslaved.

Now, vampyres gathered in the streets. Most hadn't walked in daylight since they were turned; they were wrapped in cloaks and bolstered to survive in sunlight by their new master's power.

It was a good plan, Varney thought. No one would expect vampyres to attack during the day and in the middle of the godsdamn streets!

He couldn't wait to see what the master would come up with next.

Come to think of it, Varney still didn't know the creature's name.

~ ~

KEVRIL BERSK GATHERED outside the Arkcaster church. Captain Henring followed him out and rallied a company of soldiers. For the first time since entering the city, he felt a tide of emotion shift in the soldiers. The faces of the men and women around him turned hopeful—eager—to *do something*.

Archimedes took to the sky and crowed a warning. The psychopomp felt a gathering of dark forces nearby. Bersk let his vision fade so that he could look through the eyes of the raven—

Archimedes spotted figures gathering in the alleys all throughout the city. Most were cloaked, others in plain clothes, but both the raven and the hunter saw through the ploy. All of them peered from the alleys in unison, many stalking forward in concert—their wills subjugated by force or by fear.

They were no demons—they were vampyres walking in daylight! And they looked like wolves converging for a kill.

Many were surrounding the church and the barracks, but others were spread throughout the city.

Bersk let the connection fade, and willed Archimedes to join him.

Bersk seized Captain Henring by the collar of his armor, then shouted, "Vampyres! They're coming for us." With his next breaths he cast the druid spell the *Speed of the Wind* and his goddess's spell of *Lingering Balance*.

Twitch appeared in his hand, blazing with the might of the spell. Power overflowed, causing blue ether to drip from the blade.

Throughout the city, people began to scream as the vampyres attacked indiscriminately.

Captain Henring shouted orders, sending word into the church about the attack, and ordering the men already outside to form ranks.

Henring turned to Bersk. "Where's it coming from?"

"Everywhere."

Henring's face twisted in rage. "Get the blasting powder!"

He had begun ordering the company to split in half—one to secure the city, the other to push to the river—but vampyres descended on the church. They poured from the alleys, moving with superhuman speed. They met the company of soldiers in flashes of claw and sword. Most stood their ground, hiding behind their shields, but some were thrown back, bowling over the soldiers behind them.

The Arkcaster soldiers would be strongest in the narrow streets and alleyways, where their tower shields and formations would keep them safe. All but an elder vampyre would find themselves pressed to fight in the alley. The soldiers would be most vulnerable in the open and on the wide main streets.

Bersk shoved and twisted through the ranks toward a group of five cloaked vampyres. With bolstered speed, he leapt over the front soldiers and landed between the vampyres.

Those wearing cloaks would be the youngest and trying to shield themselves from the sun. They might be deadly to a soldier, but they were nothing before Bersk's magic. With bolstered speed, he cut them down. Each would from *Twitch* flared with blue power and *Lingering Balance* burned them alive.

The company of soldiers formed a circle around the church, protecting the main entrance, but some vampyres had leapt through the side windows and ambushing those Terrans still inside.

Bersk whirled around the outside of the circle of soldiers, cutting down every vampyre he came across and skewering those wounded by the soldiers.

Then one of the cloaked vampyres met Bersk's sword with his own, and *Twitch* stopped mid-strike. The vampyre pulled back his hood and smiled like a serpent—an elder vampyre hiding amongst the young.

Bersk grit his teeth. He had known that he would come face to face with an elder vampyre, but he had hoped to have the backing of a priest or three; none of the diocese had made it outside and the regular soldiers would only slow him down.

Archimedes was only a few breaths away.

Bersk asked, "What did the demon promise you?"

"My life."

The elder vampyre slashed and Bersk parried, but the impact of the blow was too much and he was knocked backward across the street. It crossed the gap in an instant—a blur even to Bersk's heightened perception—and it was everything he could do to slip the next two strikes.

The elder was powerful, but years of unrivaled strength had made it reckless, and Bersk was able to strike with Twitch between its attacks. Three times Bersk nicked the elder before it realized its fatal mistake.

Vampyric healing was legendary: Even young vampyres could survive wounds that were fatal to most Terrans, and elder vampyres could regenerate whole limbs in a few days.

But now, the elder vampyre looked down at the wounds across its arm, midsection, and leg. They glowed with bright blue ether, and they began to spread. It gasped as it felt pain—perhaps the first it had felt for hundreds of years.

Bersk breathed easier—if the elder had been cautious, it would've been a hard battle.

Rage filled the creature's eyes. "What have you done to me!" It lunged wildly for Bersk, but the spell was already doing its work—eating away at the creature's power.

In moments, its strength and speed were less than that of a normal Terran. Bersk slashed its throat a moment later, and the elder crumpled to the ground.

A handful of cheers rose out of the company of soldiers, but more vampyres charged down the street. If they were going to make it to the river they had to go through the mass of vampyres.

Bersk shouted to the soldiers, "Captain Henring and all bound for the river, form up behind me!"

Some of the men and women hesitated, but Bersk paid them no mind. He turned to face the swarm of vampyres just as Archimedes landed beside him.

He bid Archimedes to change into its Ugu form.

The raven rustled its feathers, and then it began to grow.

~ ~

INSIDE THE INN, Tam flinched. Arkcaster erupted into chaos. Tam heard a cacophony of broken glass, stampeding feet, and all manner of screams ranging from frightened to blood-curdling.

"Come on, Tamren Jorbough." Lorith was looking at him expectantly.

Tam stared back at Lorith in disbelief. "You're mad."

"No. I have to set my misguided brethren back on the right path."

Tam looked toward the window again and the smoke rising in the distance. Whatever was going on, Bersk would be able to take care of himself. Tam didn't dare go out on his own, but maybe if he could stay close to Lorith, he could both survive *and* be useful.

Tam muttered to himself, but the words tumbled out incoherently. "Godsdamnit." Tam cleared his throat, and said, "*Primum sanctuarium.*" For the second time that day he felt the comfort of the *sanctuary* spell.

Lorith smiled, just a bit.

Tam shrugged. "After you, my lady."

~ ~

BERSK PUSHED FORWARD toward the river with the *Speed of the Wind* spell and the Arkcaster army at his back.

Bersk commanded Archimedes: *Fight through to the river.*

His connection to Archimedes faded as the raven changed. But even without seeing the psychopomp, he knew what its Ugu form looked like:

It bared a passing resemblance to a reddish brown ape, except that even hunched over its shoulders stood eight feet tall and just as wide across the chest. It weighed as much as three horses, with proportions big enough to seize a man in one hand and crush him in a breath. In stark contrast, its face was hairless, the skin taut and bone-white. Its eyes were unblinking and black. Its teeth were dagger sharp and tusks as thick as a man's arm.

Even though he no longer feel Archimedes, Bersk knew when the Ugu fully manifested by the widening eyes and collective gasps that rose around him.

The Ugu barreled past Kevril Bersk, the ground trembling beneath its knuckles. It charged like a battering ram through the vampyres. Lesser ones were caught completely by surprise and trampled underfoot.

Despite the danger, the lesser vampyres were still enthralled by the elder demon and threw themselves at the monster without care or self-preservation.

And when it was surrounded by them, it thrashed and flailed like a crazed beast—fists bigger than a man's torso killed some vampyres instantly and hurled others through walls. Its grunts of laughter echoed through the streets.

Only the older vampyres were fast enough to avoid the Ugu's rampage, but none dared get within arm's reach of the beast. So Bersk slipped through the crowd, targeting the more powerful vampyres.

Behind them, the Arkcaster army was pushing forward against the broken and the dying, mopping up and defending against their flank. They had already pushed two blocks before shouts came from behind that the Church—priests and knights—had pressed forward onto the streets to back up the other guards and brigades.

Bersk could already feel the tide turning as they pushed onward toward the river.

What felt like an hour was only a few violent moments, and they had pushed through the remaining blocks. The crowd of vampyres thinned significantly, and soldiers from the rear fanned out to flush alleyways and tend to wounded civilians.

The ambush had been quelled nearly as quickly as it appeared, but Arkcaster was far from unscathed. Wounded little the streets, and shouts of violence were replaced with wails of pain.

Then they stood at the edge of the river. Trails of smoke rose across the city, but otherwise it seemed as if the battle was over.

Captain Henring called for blasting powder and directed the soldiers to set charges at specific points over the side of the river wall. These were coated in glue and lowered over with rope doused in flammable spirits.

Three such charges were lowered over the wall and attached to the stone bank. Fuses were lit and then the soldiers pulled back.

All the while, Bersk bid the Ugu to standby in case its strength was needed. The monster crouched on its haunches, long arms setting on the ground. Most of the soldiers regarded it warily, and only a few glanced into its eyes. The Ugu paid them no mind.

"You sure this is far enough back?" Bersk asked. He'd seen blasting powder used on the Formicae hives, though those were underground and he was unaware of how much powder was used.

Henring nodded. "These men are the best. If they're standing here, then we're safe."

Arkcaster grew impossibly quiet in the final moments before the charges detonated. Explosions tore through the air and shook the ground beneath their feet.

Bersk held his breath until he heard water rushing into the newly opened hole in the catacombs. The ground shuddered again as tons of water rushed into the ancient space.

Soldiers glanced at one another, waiting to see if the ground would collapse beneath them.

Finally, Captain Henring sighed and said, "I think we're alright."

Cheers went upon from the brigade, and tepid cheers echoed throughout the city.

Then the sky turned the color of blood, and the ground rumbled as if the city would buckle and fall into the catacombs.

"What's happening?" Captain Henring shouted.

Cries echoed through the brigade and slowly the whole of them turned to see the origin of the catastrophe:

A beam of red light surrounded the Arkcaster church and rose up into the sky. From there, the color of blood seeped out toward the horizon. It felt like a great weight pressed down on the city, as if the sky had the weight of packed soil and they were being buried alive beneath it.

Henring pushed past soldiers and grabbed Bersk by the collar. "What's going on?"

"Likely the next part of the demon's ritual."

The words floated in the air, lost beneath the gravity of the moment. Even Bersk felt a tremble of hesitation against the sight of the sky.

Henring released him. "In any case it's not good."

"Agreed," Bersk replied. "Captain, we have to go back to the church."

Every ounce of sense and magic within Bersk was scream-ing at him to run—to get as far away from that beacon of death as possible. But if they did run, and the demon completely its ritual, then nowhere in the realm would be safe.

Interregnum would bleed into their realm. Demons would roam the world, free to torment the living, and Ariazi would call a second realm her own.

Slowly, Captain Henring nodded. Then he shouted to the brigade, "Form ranks! We march on the church."

~ ~ ~

Chapter 9
Crumbling Hope

SANTA ANNA HELD her tongue as Archleon Haldack banged his gavel and called for order. It was some moments before the room of normally composed men and women of the Church settled down.

She could only imagine what the other churches around the world looked like as they watched through scrying constructs at the back of the room.

"That's enough," Haldack said again. Finally, the room settled. "As I said, we will now be hearing about Santa Anna's findings in the ruins. But first, Leo Greghan, please state for the record what precautions have been taken with the findings."

Leo Greghan rose, not bothering to contain his smugness. "First, I should state that it is only with the grace of Mecendu that we were allowed to bring back records at all. They are committed to preserving the Accords between themselves and our Church.

"Second, most of the inscriptions from the ruins are embedded in stone, and so Santa Anna's records are rubbings taken from the original inscriptions. We were allowed to make two more copies of the rubbings. Each set was shipped separately and in secret to prevent tampering."

Leo Greghan turned slightly, looking at the rest of the judiciary room out of the corner of his eye. "These three copies are in our possession and await *independent translation*. Remember that when listening to Santa Anna's testimony—"

"That's enough," Archleon Haldack said from the chair. "The necessary requirements for purity are fulfilled. Santa Anna may speak freely about what she found. She knows that any misalignment of the truth will count against her.

"However, because of the sensitive nature of this information, this portion of the trial is limited to the upper diocese in attendance." Haldack motioned to the scrying constructs in the back of the room. "Disable the transmission."

Santa Anna waited while the missives disabled the scrying constructs. They were delicate works of magic and artisanship, and merely turning them off took deliberate effort.

She was thankful for the extra moments to compose herself. Anna took a deep breath.

When the constructs were off and Archleon Haldack motioned for Anna to start, the judiciary room felt much smaller.

Santa Anna said, "The ruins of Mecendu date back to the first thousand years of the Calendar of the High Mages. This is within a century of when several sections of our Enchiridion were ordained to us—notably, act six, section one.

"During my study of the ruins, I found tablets written in elvish and mecenden, as well as statues from the ancient civilizations of Hecoth and Vrace—"

"Leo Haldack," Greghan interrupted, "what bearing could this possibly have—"

"Overruled," Haldack said.

Anna continued, "I'm giving context and weight to the information I found. There are other civilizations that believed similarly to the Church of First Light, and there are overlaps between our scripture." She turned and glared at Greghan, "There are several that believe the truth of the materials I present."

Though Greghan looked irritated, he said nothing.

Anna said, "The section on the rise of the demons is incomplete. I sought answers… and I found them. There is no year given for the rise of Ariazi, no prophets have ever been powerful enough to see across millennia with exact clarity.

"But I found out *how* it happens… Ariazi's rise will be brought about by a powerful organization, and there will be a small group working inside it that will ultimately be responsible."

Murmurs spread throughout the room like fire through a dead forest. Everyone knew what she was saying: The Church's rise had been foretold—several scholars even *relished* such a prophecy—but the latter half of it had been omitted from every Church record:

Moles inside the Church of First Light would bring about the end of the world.

~ ~

TAMREN JORBOUGH FOLLOWED Lorith down the stairs and out of the inn—

Then promptly ducked back inside the doorway as two vampyres attacked her. The battle was little more than a blur, and a squelch and thumps as two mangled bodies fell to the cobbles. Lorith brushed her hair back.

But Tam paid no mind to the elder vampyre or the two dead at her feet. He was staring up at the pillar of red rising up into the sky like a whirlpool of blood. His sanctuary spell felt like a candle's warmth against a winter chill.

Tam asked, "What in Movernus's name is that?"

"The demon is opening a portal between the planes. Interregnum is bleeding into our world like blood through a fresh wound."

A chill ran down Tam's neck as the vampyre spoke. There was a mix of horror and awe in her voice.

Tam swallowed dryly. "For what it's worth, I'm glad you're on our side." The words weren't just gratitude, they were an urgent reminder. "What are we going to do?"

Lorith turned to him, her eyes fierce. "That's where we're going. Soldiers are converging on the church. We're going to help them. Try to keep up."

~ ~

BERSK AND THE Ugu led the brigade back through the streets and toward the church. It felt as if vampyres were funneling toward them from all over the city—

Coming to defend the dark ritual the elder demon had started.

Now when the vampyres swarmed them, their eyes were completely red—taken over by the demon's will. Still, Bersk silently thanked the Gray Queen that only the lesser vampyres came at them. Elder vampyres would not be subjugated so easily and it seemed they had the sense to stay far away.

By the time the church of Arkcaster came into view, Bersk was breathing heavily and his shirt was soaked with sweat. It had been a long time since he'd kept up the *Speed of the Wind* spell for so long. Though it was fueled by magic, it also tapped the body's reserves.

Bersk would be lucky if he could keep the spell up long enough to make it inside the church.

Beside him, he could feel whispers of the Ugu's weariness as well. It was a form meant for quick, decisive fights. Now Bersk had to choose between using the rest of his psychopomp's power to get to the church or save it for the fight inside the church—

Where the demon waited for them.

Reluctantly, Bersk willed Archimedes to change back. The Ugu shrank, its reddish fur flaking away. Moments later, Archimedes ruffled its feathers and took to the sky.

Their connection renewed the hunter's resolve. Archimedes felt tired and yet defiant beyond his small stature.

Bersk grinned. If Archimedes could push a little harder, then so could he.

~ ~

TAM FOLLOWED CLOSELY behind elder Lorith as she carved her way toward the church.

Only minutes ago, she'd been the epitome of control and composure. Now, her robe was torn. Her fangs were pronounced, blood dripping from them and her fingers in equal measure. She wasn't injured, not anymore. A few vampyres had managed to surround Lorith and injure her, but her injuries healed nearly as fast as they appeared.

But she was tired. Her breath was ragged and her steps haphazard.

Tam couldn't help her much—not with direct combat—but he had his luck magic. With practiced subtlety, he pushed on some enemies and pulled on others. Most thought of luck magic as paltry; admittedly, it wasn't as flashy or as powerful as evocation magic, but it was suited to battles of attrition such as this.

The other thing that Tam did to help was to stay out of the way. While Tam used luck magic, he continued holding his *sanctuary* spell. He wasn't sure exactly how it worked, but it kept most vampyres from attacking him or even noticing him at all. Which meant that Lorith didn't have to waste breath defending him. Still, he hugged the walls and dashed from building to building.

Tam had faith in the *sanctuary* spell, but it wasn't something that he was about to test.

Mercifully, they turned the final alley and stepped out in front of the church of Arkcaster—

And immediately encountered a new problem.

The glowing church was surrounded by Knights of Kripishi, their black armor and tower shields even more imposing than the ravenous vampyres.

The nearby knights saw Lorith and immediately converged on her. Lorith hissed and bared her blood-covered hands in a warning.

Tam ran past her to stand between Lorith and the knights. He spread his arms and shouted, "She is not your enemy!"

"Move out of the way!" a knight shouted.

"She's bloodlusted!"

Tam backed toward Lorith, staying between them. "We're with Kevril Bersk. We're with the church!"

Knights closed in around them. Neither Tam nor Lorith moved.

Then came shouts from the road—the same one heading toward the river. The knights stopped and spared glances in that direction.

Then a giant black bird flew between Tam and the nearest knight, squawking fiercely. The men were taken aback by it.

Tam looked toward the river and heaved a sigh of relief. Bersk had arrived. He jogged toward them, his sword, *Twitch*, out in fearsome display.

Bersk looked from Lorith to Tam, then turned to face the knights. "I am Kevril Bersk. I fight for the Order, and these two are with me." A few of the men looked uneasily to Lorith, but stood down.

From behind them, Captain Henring and Commander Zin shouted for the soldiers to form ranks. The Commander clutched a reddened cloth to his chest while pushing away a soldier trying to tend to him.

Bersk smiled with faint relief as the knights turned around. "Glad you made it."

Tam shrugged. "We ran into some trouble, but nothing that Lorith and I—well, Lorith, couldn't handle."

Lorith turned to Bersk. "We must hurry. The longer his ritual goes on, the more vampyres will come to his air."

Bersk met her eyes. "You don't have to come in with us."

Tam turned to Lorith. He knew what Bersk meant—they all did. If she was inside when the ritual reached its peak, then Lorith would lose control of herself just like the lesser vampyres.

Lorith shook her head, her eyes defiant. "I've hid for too long. This is my city. This is my realm. Not *his*."

Bersk said, "The Knights of Kripishi will go in first, and we'll be in the center of them. Keep your wits about you." Bersk hesitated, as if he wanted to say more.

Tam knew this too. He put a hand on his friend's shoulder. "We'll keep our wits about us."

Bersk nodded. Then Archimedes flew to his shoulder and the hunter led them into the waiting muster of knights.

~ ~ ~

Chapter 10
Into the Abyss

ARCHLEON HALDACK HAD trouble maintaining order. The crowd in the judiciary room had devolved into shouting.

Santa Anna stood tall, despite most of the shouting being meant for her.

Finally, a deafening shout echoed through the room. *"ENOUGH!"*

Columen Devery had amplified his voice and the very room trembled before his magic. The chandeliers above rattled and the paintings on the wall shook. Everyone in attendance flinched and quickly took their seats again.

And then Devery waved a hand for the trial to continue.

Archleon Haldack turned to Santa Anna. "As you were saying."

Santa Anna continued, unperturbed, "Those are the extent of my findings. I move immediately for the creation of a special counsel to investigate the diocese—everyone Archleon and higher."

Again, the judiciary room threatened to break into chaos, but Archleon Haldack shouted over all of them for order.

As soon as the volume ebbed, Leo Greghan spoke up. "This is absurd! She is completely unfounded in these accusations. She cites that Mecendu and others fear our Church, as well they should! They are jealous of our prosperity. Such accusations only serve to destabilize what we've worked so hard to achieve."

Anna retorted, "Do you deny the rise of the Desolate Family in Arkcaster at this very moment?"

"Until it is confirmed, it is nothing more than an elder demon, something that is unfortunate and not worthy of debate."

"But what if it is?" Anna asked.

Greghan stiffened. "There is a reason that the prophets and pillars compiled the Enchiridion as they did, and it is sacrilegious of me to contradict them." He turned to Archleon Haldack, as if that concluded the exchange, but Anna wasn't finished.

"It behooves us to investigate the claims. So many civilizations cannot be wrong in their wisdom of the rise of demons, even if it contradicts our scripture."

All eyes fell expectantly to Archleon Haldack, who carefully considered the arguments. The room grew utterly quiet as the moment dragged on.

Finally, Haldack said, "It is the decision of this court that we will take all manner of evidence presented with the utmost gravity. I shall convene with the diocese to create a special counsel to investigate our ranks." When mumblings of disagreement rose, so did Haldack's voice. "Our Church is above the petty disagreements of our ranks. We must endure, and if that means we must exorcize a tumor from our midst, then we will do so with the decisiveness of an executioner's axe."

Leo Greghan waited for Haldack to finish before he seethed, "So long as the special counsel starts with her!"

Archleon Haldack's irritation slowly crawled into a smirk. "I think that's what this is, Greghan. Santa Anna has already put herself before the scrutiny of the diocese. I believe you've just volunteered to be second."

Leo Greghan collapsed to his chair, finally—thankfully—silenced.

Anna felt the smallest sense of satisfaction. One that quickly gave way to trepidation. In a quiet way, she had hoped to be wrong—that some other evidence would come to light that there weren't moles within their ranks and that the Church of First Light wasn't to blame for the possible apocalypse.

Anna spoke up, forcing herself to speak loud enough to hear. "I implore the Church—all of you—to take this information to heart. Even if our branch in Arkcaster succeeds in stopping the Desolate Family there, the fight will only be just beginning. We must unite against the enemies from outside and those from within."

But even as her voice rose over the murmurs of the room, Santa Anna felt doubt in their stares.

The Church of First Light was already divided.

She had to hope that the translators would prove her right, and that truth would be enough to rally the diocese together.

~ ~

THE KNIGHTS OF Kripishi cast spells of strength and willpower on themselves. Others cast their armor with wards and their swords in the spell of fire.

Bersk checked his armor and turned to the vampyre Lorith. She was staring at the church with a far off look in her eyes.

Bersk recognized that look—the vampyre was preparing herself for the horrors to come.

Bersk asked, "Would you take magic?"

Lorith startled and then nodded.

"I can't promise how much it would do for one who already had your power," Bersk said, "but it might help steady your mind." Then he cast the spell of strength on himself, Lorith, and Tam.

He might've stretched the spell further, but so many knights and soldiers were already laden with magic, and too many spells couldn't layer on top of one another.

Lorith sighed and already seemed to breathe easier. She admired her sharpened nails. "It's been a long time since I felt such potent magic. I admit, I miss the feeling… You must have a powerful benefactor."

Archimedes crowed with satisfaction, but Bersk didn't answer. He recast the spell of *Lingering Balance* on *Twitch*. The color of the magic sword brightened and ether resumed dripping from the blade.

Commander Zin called for them to join the ranks. The old man had staunched his wound and had finally seen to the attention of a medic. The young man carefully dressed the commander's shoulder while he yelled out battle plans.

The red light that swallowed the church of Arkcaster was growing—not just higher into the sky but wider as well. In minutes, it was reaching out to the surrounding city block.

They were out of time.

And the church had lost many of its priests and the archleon in the initial attack. Now, the few priests that remained would follow behind Bersk's group

Then the first knights charged the doors of the church and shoved them open. Bersk, Archimedes, Lorith, and Tam went through after the first squad.

The view inside was nauseating, even with Bersk's spell of strength. One knight in front vomited in the corner. Bersk and his group walked past.

The inside of the church was bathed in the same red light. The walls were now made of bricks of bone and marrow for mortar. The once marbled floor was now made of bone, like the spine of some buried monster. Bersk swore he heard the dull beating of the heart somewhere in those walls.

To the right, the body of a priest sat in an alcove—split open like a grisly bouquet; the only recognizable part of them was the remains of their hat and robe.

Another knight wretched behind them, either from the sights or from the growing smell of sulfur and blood.

Bersk nearly glanced backward to check on Tam and Lorith, but he didn't dare take his eyes off the halls—the spells would have to be enough for them.

Beyond the faint beating of the walls came the patter of feet. Knights and soldiers shouted orders, but even these sounded faint—muffled by the red glow.

Lesser demons spilled in from the side halls, leaping like hairless apes at the knights. They crashed into shields, were slashed open by swords, and burst into flames as they were repelled by the magic of the Order.

Flashes of bright yellow light illuminated the hall, some sailing over Bersk's shoulder—*Hard Light Spears*. Weapons of the priests brought to bear. Like radiant lightning bolts, they homed in on demons, spearing two or three at a time and bursting them.

Together, their formation pushed into the twisted heart of Arkcaster church.

A horrid sound echoed through the church—even through the muted halls. The patter of a hundred feet and choked screams.

An amalgamation turned the corner of the hall and it was no longer the slow loping form from the catacombs. Now it was bolstered by the elder demon's magic and the realm of Interregnum.

The centipedal wall of flesh *galloped* toward them, its every undulation sending tremors through the church. Its limbs bled with the force of each impact, but pain only spurred the monster.

Bersk pushed forward to the knights in front, calling for *strength* and *flame*.

In the wide hallways, Bersk and three knights stood shoulder to shoulder, shields raised. Four more knights placed their shields against their backs to buttress them.

The amalgamation's screams rose like a whirlwind, drowning out the frantic cries of the knights and soldiers. Men ducked behind their shields.

The monster slammed into them, sending all eight men skidding backward across the spine of the floor. Bersk kept his shoulder against his shield and stabbed over it desperately, plunging *Twitch* into the beast over and over. The front three knights did the same.

Somewhere distant, Bersk heard frantic shouts as more of their squad backpedaled or tripped and were crushed underfoot.

Only when the front of the amalgamation was consumed by fire and dripping blue ether did it stop. Then the knights shoved.

Together they heaved, pushing back with the strength of dozens of men, shoving the monster back and then using the newfound gap to slash and rend it with their swords. Lances of hard light shot over their shoulders, carving swathes off the top of the monster.

Someone—Lorith—called out to hold. Bersk saw her run down a side hall with several soldiers.

The air grew thick with blood, screams, and burning flesh. Bersk's shield was covered in gore and all he could think of was *forward*.

Then a roar rose through the church—a cacophony of screams. The amalgamation buckled, twisting and writhing backward down the hall.

Bersk and the knights redoubled their efforts, carving sections out of the beast as they pushed forward. With every step, the creature's strength sagged.

When they had carved halfway through it, they met Lorith. She was covered in red, having flanked the amalgamation from the side and torn into it with vampyric strength.

She nodded to Bersk, then let the knights pass.

Together, they pushed into the heart of Arkcaster church.

~

The Knights of Kripishi pushed into what used to be the congregation room in the back of the church.

Where the halls had been mixtures of brick and gore, nearly all remnants of the church were gone. It wasn't even a twisted mirror of the Church's opulence.

Chandeliers were replaced with spiderwebs and sinew. Tapestries of light and order were replaced with flayed skin. The walls were fibrous muscle that rose and fell like they were breathing. The floor writhed beneath their feet, as if they were walking on the back of an enormous beast.

Demons crawled through the rafters and along the walls, tearing bleeding chunks out of the new church.

And in the center of it all stood a bone altar.

It rose up to the ceiling—a twisting sculpture of bone. Bersk's eyes lingered on the structure, his heart and stomach feeling like they were twisting and tumbling in his chest.

Altars of Ariazi were profane things that sickened all creatures not from the plane of Interregnum. But this…

It was a sculpture, Bersk realized—not merely a structure. Wisdom said that Altars of Ariazi were scars on their realm, bled over from the realm of the demons. In that sense, they were more akin to natural phenomena, like mountain ranges or trees.

This altar had form and regularity to it, like the facade of a church lovingly crafted by a master.

It was… beautiful. And as the thought occurred to Bersk, he suppressed a gag.

"Do not be afraid."

A thing approximating a man stepped around the altar and faced the knights. Such an unassuming frame. Its face had filled out since Bersk saw it last.

The demon spoke warmly. "You who seek and serve the Light, should be afraid least of all. You who follow blindly should be the first to see the glory of my mother—mother of all demons. Yes… We have use for you. All rulers need an army, at least for a while." Then its voice turned cold. "There is still time to repent. Throw yourselves before the altar."

No Terrans took their eyes off the demon. The knights in front uttered a *bulwark* spell and raised their shields. Bersk kept hold of his *strength* and *lingering balance*.

Wordlessly, the Knights of Kripishi pushed forward, fanning out into the twisted congregation room.

The demon didn't move. "On your knees or on your feet, you will atone with pain. *YOU'RE MINE TO CONTROL.*"

Before the demon finished his spell, Bersk was already exchanging strength for *Speed of the Wind* and extending the spell to Tam and as many of the surrounding soldiers as he could.

Lorith screamed, and the soldiers in the hall turned to face her. The vampyre trembled as she fought to remain in control of herself.

Bersk barely saw her first attack. She swung back, his hand pulverizing one knight's head and helmet. He slumped to the ground as the others converged on her.

Bersk leapt in front of Tam, shouting for him to get back, but they were trapped in the tight confines of the hallway with an elder vampyre. There was nowhere to run.

At the same time, Bersk willed Archimedes to change back into its Ugu form. He had to hope that the psychopomp's strength and several frontline knights would be enough to distract the demon.

Lorith lunged for Bersk and he met her strikes with Twitch. The blade seared through her knuckles, but each strike forced Bersk backward and finally against the wall. Tam was knocked off his feet and slumped down against the corner of the hall.

Twice more, Lorith slashed at him before turning against the other knights. Even though her hands were dripping with blue wounds, she still cut clean through the breastplates of two men—the metal screeching and then clanking on the floor.

She missed another knight while yet another slashed across her back.

It was then that Bersk felt the subtle nudges of chance from Tam. Even though he was still on the floor, he was determined to help.

The hallway became a maelstrom of violence. For every knight or soldier that managed to land a blow, Lorith gutted another. Even with enhanced speed, most men were no match for an elder vampyre. It was likely that Lorith's was still fighting for influence and struggling *not to kill them all.*

Impacts sounded from the congregation room, like trees being felled. Bersk spared a glance to the room to see the Ugu swinging wildly while both the demon and the knights hurled magic at one another. The demon seemed to be dodging the psychopomp, but it clearly didn't know what to make of the Ugu's magic resistance.

It would've been a humorous thing, if not for Bersk's current predicament. The demon clearly meant to win without dirtying its hands, but no magic could affect the Ugu—none of this realm, Interregnum, or any other.

Bersk turned back to the task at hand and redoubled his efforts. He whirled around behind Lorith and slashed her across the back.

Eventually, every attack from the *lingering balance* spell would weaken her—if the demon's concentration didn't break first.

Lorith turned for Bersk, and he again felt the subtle nudges of luck aiding his blade and saving his neck.

Then Lorith's eyes cleared.

Rather than turn and run, she leapt directly at Bersk—at *Twitch*. The blue sword impaled her, and Bersk felt her strength fade as she slumped to the ground. Bersk knelt beside her, sword still in hand—

But Lorith's eyes were still clear. "Go," she said. "Go finish it."

"Go," Tam added, pushing himself to his feet.

Bersk turned and ran past the few knights in the hallway that were still able to fight, and ran into the congregation room.

The elder demon stood in the middle of the room, surrounded by enemies, and he toyed with them. With gestures, he brushed aside sword strikes and sidestepped magic blasts. Even the Ugu, with all its might, couldn't land a direct blow. The demon brushed aside its massive fists and the room shuddered beneath each missed strike.

"It's futile," the demon said casually—without even a hint of malice. "There is no stopping what we've set in motion."

Bersk sprinted forward with the *Speed of the Wind* and slipped between the knights and the Ugu. Thrice he caught the demon unaware; blue slashes appeared on the demon's back and shoulder—

And they faded. *It had overpowered the spell of Lingering Order.*

The demon's calm demeanor finally slipped. It lunged for Bersk and he slipped away.

The Ugu stepped between them, defending Bersk. Then the demon grabbed the Ugu's next punch—stopping it cold—and hurled the psychopomp across the room. The Ugu slammed into the far way, shaking the foundation beneath their feet.

Bersk changed his spells. He called upon his spell of strength so that he wouldn't be killed outright, and then he called upon one of his goddess's forbidden spells: *"Vetiti ordinis: Orrorim effigies."*

The man that was Kevril Bersk became many. Ten copies of him appeared throughout the room—all wearing the same enchanted armor and wielding *Twitch.*

They descended on the demon and it met them with a sneer. Its calm facade was gone completely, its face twisting from man to snarling beast from one moment to the next. But scarier than its flickering exterior was its power.

It turned aside the strikes of knights, Bersk, and Ugu alike—fighting twenty bolstered men and a monster like they were children. Worse, even with Berk's strength, the impacts wrenched his arm and sent each copy of himself sliding back.

One by one, Bersk's magic faltered and his copies winked out.

They couldn't win—not like this.

So one of Bersk's copies slinked away behind the altar and sent to scrawling sigils in the bones. It wouldn't completely erase the altar, but it would buy them time to retreat and re-group.

Bersk etched the ancient designs into the structure and the altar of bone began to rumble.

But before he finished, Bersk felt several things all at once. He felt the Ugu's pain as it was hurled across the room and the last of its strength faded. He felt the last of his mirror copies disappear. Heard the screams of the last knights—

And he felt a hand at his throat.

With one hand, the elder demon lifted Bersk off the ground by his neck. The hunter slashed at the creature with *Twitch*, but the blue blade didn't cut or even scratch it.

The demon's flesh writhed beneath the skin, as if its muscles were alive with minds of their own.

"There is a poetry in this," the demon said, its face once again a mask of calm blankness. "That the Church's greatest weapon escaped their grasp. Yet you still fight for them—would still die for them."

"No," Bersk muttered. He let Twitch fade and held the demon's wrist so he wouldn't pass out.

"What was that, Kevril Bersk?"

"I don't fight for them. I… I fight for the Gray Queen."

"Yes, yes. The absent goddess. No matter." The demon's eyes widened, and then narrowed on Bersk. "My mother offers you one final time, fight for her, and your suffering in the new world will be ecstasy instead of a nightmare."

Bersk groaned, his hands slipping on the demon's wrist. His vision was swimming, and he heard no sounds of anyone else alive in the room.

He only hoped that Tam had the sense to run…

Because Bersk had one final hope—one last card to play. And he had no idea if it would work.

Bersk said, "I call upon the Dead Prince."

The demon smiled, but before it could speak, a tear opened in the world with the sound of thunder—

The wall behind them split from floor to ceiling, the red flesh of the walls giving way to a blinding light.

From the light stepped an owl shaped creature, fifteen feet tall with feathers white and shining as fresh snow. Its beak was split so that it resembled interlocking fangs, and a crown of antlers adorned its head. Its eyes were black as gemstones.

The Dead Prince stepped through the tear and roared— half shriek and half earth-rumbling bellow.

The demon dropped Bersk and turned. It stared wide-eyed, blood pouring down its cheeks.

Before the demon could move again, the Dead Prince lunged. The Dead Prince pinned the demon to the floor with one enormous foot, its talons splitting the bones of the floor.

Bersk was thrown across the room by its wings and slammed into the wall. Archimedes—still drained from battle—cooed and leapt into his arms. Bersk clutched the raven. His eyes burned and he could feel blood streaming from them, but no matter how desperately he wanted to close them, Bersk couldn't look away—

Not until judgment was passed.

The Prince spoke in a voice older than their realm—one Bersk only understood because he was bound to the Gray Queen.

"Belial, first born of Ariazi, you are banished to the realm of Inter-regnum. You are not welcome here."

White light flared and thunder cracked. A wave of hot wind washed over Bersk, and the blood on his face dried instantly. The room and his vision turned blindingly white.

When the light faded, Bersk still couldn't close his eyes.

In the center of the twisted congregation room, where the demon had been only moments before, Interregnum had been erased. The muscle of the walls and bone of the floor had been erased at the point of judgment, returning the normal wood, pews, and altar. It was a solemn sight amidst the demonic realm that still lingered in the rest of the room.

The Dead Prince turned to Kevril Bersk, and it came for him. It walked over, each step shaking the building and its talons gouging chunks out of the floor.

It stopped in front of Bersk and looked down on him.

"Kevril Bersk, servant of the Gray Queen, your call was inevitable and there is no penance required. You will continue to serve our Queen. She is not done with you."

With the Prince's decree, Bersk was free. He shut his eyes in pain and thanks and reverence as the right hand of his goddess walked through the tear in the world and then vanished.

~ ~ ~

Chapter 11
Aftermath
in the Light

ARCHIMEDES HOPPED AWAY and Bersk pushed himself to his feet. His legs trembled and the dried blood on his face cracked. Fresh tears fell from his eyes, both from the searing pain they'd just been subjected to and that he was still alive.

To call upon the Dead Prince for an unworthy cause condemned the summoner to death.

Granted, he was pretty sure the rise of the Son of Ariazi and the coming of the demons was a worthy cause, but to look upon the Dead Prince and live to tell the tale was not something many could attest to.

Bersk shook off his delirium and walked to the demonic altar. He still had one final job to do.

He knelt in front of the bones, conjured *Twitch*, and scrawled the necessary sigils into the floor. Lesser demons screamed from the rafters but Bersk paid them no mind, and they didn't dare come down to the floor to attack him—not because of Bersk, but because of the presence left by the Prince.

When Bersk finished, he held his sword out over the sigils and spoke the old words.

"By the will of the Gray Queen, I am her hand and her voice.

"I stand upon the shoulders of the Dead Prince,

"Spurned by the Realm That Has No Name.

"We impose the Balance upon this cursed land."

When he spoke the final line, two other voices overlapped his, and Kevril Bersk knew he was not alone.

Blue ether dripped from the sword, filling the design with molten magic. His sword turned to dull steel as the magic of the Gray Queen took hold.

"By the will of the Gray Queen, erase this madness," the three voices said.

The church of Arkcaster rumbled and the muscles and bones of Interregnum twisted around him. Blue oozed from the bone altar, splitting the structure apart. In moments, the whole of it crumbled to the ground and the realm of Interregnum faded around Bersk, leaving stone and wood in its wake. The lesser demons hiding in the rafters burst out of existence.

Blue ether leapt from the sigils back to his sword.

"Order come, and Gray Queen's will be done."

Beside him, Archimedes crowed with satisfaction, and Bersk willed away the magic sword. Then he heaved a sigh of relief and turned back to the others.

The inside of Arkcaster church was in ruins; pews and decorations were splintered, windows were shattered. Bersk ignored it all.

Tam was propped up against the corner of the hallway, wiping dried blood from his eyes. Soldiers were stirring around him and seeing to their wounded. Two wept quietly. They all shared the same bleeding eyes.

Mortals were not meant to look upon the old gods.

Bersk eyed several soldiers, but didn't stop. Most were already dead, including Captain Henring; Bersk winced; the once stoic man lay in an unmoving heap.

Bersk said a silent prayer for the captain, then went to Tam and patted him on the shoulder.

Tam startled, as if shaken from a trance. "Bersk—I…" He turned and half-crawled, half-crouched to Lorith. She laid motionless, but was breathing softly. Her wounds no longer glowed with blue ether.

"Will she be alright?" Tam asked.

Bersk knelt down and checked her wounds. Her bleeding had all but stopped and the shallower cuts were already healing. Aside from some specks of blood, her face was unmarred—she hadn't seen the Prince.

Bersk nodded. "I think she'll be fine."

Tam smirked but looked as if he was fighting back tears. "I don't want to see any more of your tricks, Bersk. I've seen more in the past few weeks than I have in all the other years. What… What was that you summoned?"

"That was the Dead Prince, vassal of the Gray Queen."

"I didn't want to look… but I couldn't shut my eyes."

"I know." Bersk offered his friend a hand and pulled him to his feet. Tam stood uneasily, but he stood.

Tam asked, "*That's* whose name you invoke when you cleanse the altars?"

"One of them, yes."

Shouts sounded from down the hall. Knights and soldiers pushed through the church. From the back, Commander Zin shouted for them to cordon off the area and take stock of the wounded.

The Church and the army could take it from here. With any luck, his job was ending.

~ ~

VARNEY BARRIS SKULKED through the back alleys of Arkcaster and scratched at the scabs of his wounds. He'd been slashed across the stomach and thigh and the wounds hadn't healed right—he blamed it on the flaming swords that bastards had used. Some holy spell or another.

Hurt like the piss.

Varney had half a mind to run after the first time he got cut, but he'd fought the good fight. He'd been a good little vampyre.

Then the red beacon had fallen.

He knew—he *knew* that it was over. He could feel it in his undead bones: The demon lost. How in the name of all things unholy that happened, Varney didn't know, but he sure as shit wasn't staying around to find out.

Some of the Knights might recognize him, might search the blood dens for him. Shit—they might just clean out the blood dens for revenge. The Church wouldn't care that most of the vampyres were enthralled and had no choice.

More of those knights would come. More of the priests. They would come—Varney knew.

They might even bring a saint with them.

He'd leave Arkcaster at nightfall. Yes. Out the front gate or over the wall. Either way, he wasn't staying in Arkcaster another night.

~ ~

SOLDIERS, KNIGHTS, AND priests worked together to take care of the wounded in the battle for Arkcaster church.

Bersk waited to confer with Commander Zin, Columen Jonn, and Pater Lurecine. He told them of the battle, of Belial, and the judgment of the Gray Queen. This last piece was met with mixes of disdain and outrage, neither of which Bersk entertained. He reminded them to send word to Septriones and the rest of the Church, and thankfully they didn't pursue it further.

But the Church moved too slowly for Kevril Bersk.

By the time they were ready to leave, Elder Lorith could stand on her own. Bersk and Tam helped her slip away back to *Les Enfants Terribles*. They walked down the stairs and took her all the way to the door.

On shaky feet, Lorith pushed herself inside and found the den in as much disarray as the city above. Furniture and decorations were strewn about and dried blood coated the ground, but there were no bodies.

The den was completely empty.

"Gods," Tam muttered. "What happened here?"

"Nothing that can't be undone," Lorith replied. She limped over to a chair and sat. "Thank you."

Bersk nodded. "You shouldn't stay here. The Church will take any excuse to come for you." It was only through an uneasy truce that the blood dens and vampyres were allowed to exist at all.

"I think they'll see to reason," she said.

"Why's that?"

"Because now they've seen what open war would look like, and it didn't go too well for them."

The Church would bring more… Bersk shook his head. He knew she wouldn't see to reason.

"Be careful," Bersk finally said, then turned to leave.

"Kevril Bersk… May I never see you again."

Bersk and Tam left *Les Enfants Terribles*. They exited the stairs into the alleyway.

"Lovely woman," Tam said sarcastically, as if surprised by her change of heart.

Bersk shrugged. "You'd be surprised how often I get that sentiment."

Bersk and Tam walked back to the inn, where Bersk barred the door. Just because the battle was done·didn't mean that the city was completely safe now.

"I have to go to Septriones," Bersk said.

"I know," Tam replied. He made a show of holding his sore arm as he sat down on the bed. Flecks of dried blood still lingered around his eyes. "Go on. I'll be right here."

~

Kevril Bersk used his lodestone to return to Septriones chuch on the other side of the world.

One moment, he was standing next to Tam. The next, he was standing in Pater O'Malley's empty study.

Bersk walked quickly through the halls to the main floor of Septriones, where he joined with a group of priests and knights who were awaiting the final verdicts of Santa Anna's trial. It seemed that the scrying constructs had been disabled for the last hours while the court discussed sensitive information.

It was another hour before the trial concluded and a mass of diocese came down the grand stairs.

Santa Anna was in the center, still in manacles. She was flanked by others, including Columen Devery and Archleon Greghan.

None of them saw Bersk, or stopped to answer any questions. They merely paraded Anna past, presumably to take her back to the holding cell.

Bersk's heart sank. Surely they would see her innocence! Surely...

"Bersk!"

The hunter turned to find Pater O'Malley. The wiry priest clasped him by the shoulders and ushered him out the doors and into the gardens.

"Are you alright?" O'Malley asked. "Is Tamren alright?"

"Yes, yes," Bersk replied, waving the priest away.

"We got word of Belial. We'd been about to adjourn when we got the news... Sorry." O'Malley straightened his robe and sighed. "The Church is still digesting the news."

"What's the verdict?"

O'Malley's eyes widened, as if he'd forgotten entirely about Santa Anna's trial. "Oh! Yes. She's been found righteous. It took the diocese a while to—"

"Then why is she still in chains?" Bersk asked.

"They're still figuring out what to do with her."

Bersk stuttered, "What—What? She's been found righteous and she was investigating the very prophecies that have come to pass! What more is there to discuss?"

O'Malley grasped Bersk firmly by the shoulders. "Easy, Bersk. *She's been found righteous.* The rest is formalities. She'll be out of manacles by this evening."

Slowly, Bersk nodded. "Good. What's the next steps?"

"Well, the Church is going to renew Santa Anna's investigation. They're opening up conversation lines with Mecendu as we speak. With any luck, they will allow us access to the ruins."

Bersk breathed a sigh of relief. That was a quicker and better response that he'd expected. Perhaps he'd been too hard on the Church.

Something O'Malley said caught his attention. "What do you mean *us?*"

O'Malley replied, "The Church is sending a team of knights and priests to the ruins."

"Good, for a minute I thought you meant that you and I were going." When the priest didn't say anything right away, Bersk said, "Out with it, Pater."

"Columen Devery is requisitioning your service. You, myself, and Santa Anna. We'll be given our own team. Of course, Tam will be offered a spot as well."

Bersk stifled his optimism and eyed his former seigneur suspiciously. "To do what?"

O'Malley shrugged and pointed across the gardens and toward the holding cells. "We better catch up. Columen Devery will want to tell you himself."

~

O'Malley and Bersk walked quickly and caught up to the small procession led by Columen Devery, Archleon Greghan, and Santa Anna. They followed in silence through the gardens to the sepulcher, then down the stone stairs to the holding rooms beneath.

It wasn't until they were in the torchlight of the central chamber that Columen Devery produced the small key that released Santa Anna's bonds.

She rubbed her wrists and thanked him.

Leo Greghan turned to take stock of everyone's attendance, then cleared his throat. "Now, if you're satisfied, Devery, we should discuss the matter at hand."

Columen Devery's smile didn't waver. "It is important that the Church looks into the prophecies that Santa Anna uncovered in the ruins of Mecendu. But we have even more pressing concerns."

Devery produced a copy of the Enchiridion from the shelves and opened it on the desk before him. "Others of the Desolate Family will be coming in the wake of the Son. Some of them are already here." He read aloud, "The Witchpawn are twisted mirrors of the Mother of Demons. It is through them that Ariazi sees and through them she will plot her way to the mortal realm."

Silence hung in the air. It was Pater O'Malley who broke it. "Do you know where they are?"

"I do," Santa Anna replied quietly.

Devery said, "Part of the prophecies she discovered told of the location of the Witchpawn. They're deep in the Eastern jungles of Ozequn."

Greghan grumbled, "Prophecies are well and good, Devery, but hardly worth a mission on the other side of the world."

"I've seen them," Devery responded curtly. "The Columen pooled our power through one of the long range scrying stones. They're right where Santa Anna's prophecies put them."

Bersk crossed his arms. "What do you have planned, Columen? And why do you need us?"

Devery smirked. "Isn't it obvious? We need knights and priests—capable ones. You, Pater O'Malley, and Santa Anna will lead a team through the jungle. You're to find the Witchpawn, and dispose of them. Without her eyes and her gateway… perhaps we can thwart Ariazi's return."

"But you're not certain." Bersk replied. "What if there are other prophecies that say otherwise?"

Santa Anna put a hand on Bersk's shoulder. "It's our best plan. You trusted us once. Trust us again."

Bersk felt both uncomfortable and emboldened by her touch. Even if her hand was on his armor, it felt as if she saw right through him.

"Okay," Bersk finally said. "I trust you."

You. Not them.

~ ~ ~

Epilogue
Ripples

KEVRIL BERSK, SANTA Anna, and Pater O'Malley stood on the docks of Fairweather. The morning sun was still rising in the sky, but the docks were already bustling.

No one was near them however. It seemed as if most of the sailors wanted to stay clear of the Church and the ships that took on their commission.

All the better, Bersk thought as he breathed the salty air. It'd been too long since he'd traveled by boat—he'd journeyed across the world more times than most would ever dream of in a lifetime, all thanks to the Church's lodestone.

But some places had to be gotten to the old-fashioned way.

"It will be quicker to sail," Columen Devery said beside them. He smiled broadly as he looked out over the sea and at the *Satyr* docked in front of them. "The Church doesn't have any lodestone anchors within two hundred miles of the jungle. Better to go by sea."

The Columen spared a glance at Bersk and Santa Anna, and Bersk's face flushed.

After all, Bersk wasn't just looking forward to spending time at sea. It had been too long since he'd spoken with Anna, and waiting idly on the docks pained him.

The coming of Interregnum had been stopped and they were safe, if only for a moment. Bersk had every intention of making it last and enjoying it.

END

Note about *The Sword of the Gray Queen*

This concludes the first arc of the series.

I've been working on the Eluthiya dark fantasy universe since 2020, and while there are other stories planned in the universe, I won't be releasing them as quickly as I have the last two and a half years.

A Battleaxe and a Metal Arm is complete, and *Tales from Another World* and *The Sword of the Gray Queen* will be on a tentative schedule as of March 2023.

There are still other stories to tell, but I've finished this arc and tried to leave Bersk, Santa Anna, and Tam on *a happy for now* instead of happily ever after.

Thank you for following the series so far, and hopefully I'll have good new in the near future.

The End...
For now

Thank you for Reading

I hope you enjoyed reading this story as much as I enjoyed writing it.

If you did, I would massively appreciate a short review on Amazon or your favorite book website. Reviews are crucial for any author, and a starred review or even just a line or two can make a huge difference.

It's especially true for the start of a series. Thanks and I hope you enjoy the next one!

Looking for more dark fantasy stories in this universe?

The Sword of the Gray Queen is one series in a dark fantasy universe, *Eluthiya*.

Tales from Another World is an ongoing short story series containing stories about sorcerers, druids, mortals, gods, thieves, and all other manner of Terrans from all over the twin continents.

Among other stories, will be snippets of Sircius Everdeath's crusade that nearly destroyed the world! So, if you're interested, be sure to check out the ongoing series.

And if you liked the action and adventure in this story, be sure to check out the ongoing monthly serial **A Battleaxe and a Metal Arm.** It's the adventure of a lifetime… or several!

About the Sword of the Gray Queen

So, if you've read this far, you're probably curious about the origins of this story. Hopefully you read the back matter in The Sword of the Gray Queen 1.

It all came from a fan fiction idea: The Witches Kills Cereal Box Mascots.

The first installment was supposed to be Geralt going up against the Honey Smacks Dig 'Em Frog.

The second installment was a hive full of Honey Nut Cheerios Bees.

This installment was Count Chocula!

Connect with the Author

If you want to stay up to date on the latest about Samuel's publishing news and blog, check out his website and consider signing up for his monthly newsletter.

www.SamuelFlemingBooks.com

Samuel can also be found on Reddit, Tiktok, and Facebook.

Samuel Fleming is a Science Fiction and Fantasy author.

He grew up in Maryland, spending most of his time swimming and writing. Swimming gave him a lot of time to daydream, so the two hobbies complemented each other well. Idle day dreams turned into stories, some of which stuck with him for years. These days he swims a little less and writes a lot more.

He loves a good story no matter the medium: Books, TV, video games, comics, tabletop RPG's, or podcasts—most of which he attempts to share with his wife and three kids, and occasionally on his blog.